BEWARE THE NINJA WEENIES

AND OTHER WARPED AND CREEPY TALES

BEWARE THE NINJA WEENIES

AND OTHER WARPED AND CREEPY TALES

DAVID LUBAR

A TOM DOHERTY ASSOCIATES BOOK
NEW YORK

BEWARE THE NINJA WEENIES

Copyright © 2012 by David Lubar

Reader's Guide copyright © 2012 by Tor Books

All rights reserved.

A Starscape Book
Published by Tom Doherty Associates, LLC
175 Fifth Avenue
New York, NY 10010

www.tor-forge.com

ISBN 978-0-7653-3213-4

First Edition: June 2012

Printed in the United States of America

0   9   8   7   6   5   4   3   2   1

For Susan Chang, editor, friend, and advocate.
Thanks for working so hard to make me look good.

CONTENTS

CONTENTS

BEWARE THE NINJA WEENIES AND OTHER WARPED AND CREEPY TALES

PLAYING SOLO

Henry fired a mortar round at the cluster of aliens. Perfect! It hit their group dead center, and blew them up in a geyser of brown soil and green flesh.

"Nice!" Stan said. "I'll flank the other squadron while you distract them."

"Got it," Henry said into the microphone of his headset. He pushed the right thumb stick to rotate the camera toward the other group of enemies. Then he tapped the D-pad to switch weapons. No use wasting mortar shells. He fired short bursts from his plasma rifle, knocking chips of stone off the broken statues that sheltered the enemy. They responded by sending a hail of blind fire in his direction.

"Almost there," Stan said.

Henry panned the camera back, but couldn't spot his friend.

"As soon as you attack, I'll move closer," he said. "Okay?"

Instead of answering, Stan screamed, "Aliens!"

"Ouch! Stop that." Henry lowered the volume. "Of course there are aliens. That's the whole point of this game—to fight the aliens."

11

"No. Real ones!" Stan yelled.

Henry rotated the view all the way around until he got back to the starting point. He didn't see anything that hadn't been there before. No new enemies had shown up on the radar map, either.

"Aaggggg! *Noooo!*"

A message scrolled across the top of the screen.

CONNECTION LOST. STANROCKS720 HAS DROPPED OUT.

"Very funny," Henry muttered. He had no idea why Stan had quit, but he was happy to play the game by himself. He switched back to the mortar, slipped closer, and took out the second group of aliens with another perfectly placed shot. Then he headed over the ridge, where he suspected he'd find ammo crates and health pickups.

"I knew it," he said when he saw the stockpile of supplies. Now that he had full health and plenty of ammo, he decided to keep going. According to the walk-through he'd checked before starting this session, there were only five levels left. It would serve Stan right if he missed out on the ending.

Half an hour later, Henry felt someone tugging on his sleeve. "Can I play?" his little brother, Ruben, asked.

"Go away." Even if Ruben had any chance of lasting more than five seconds in the game without getting vaporized by an energy whip or blown to pieces by an omega mine, Henry wasn't going to put up with a split screen, which was the only option for two players on the same console.

"Please . . ." Ruben said.

"I mean it," Henry said. "Go away!"

Ruben stormed off. Henry didn't even look up. He couldn't care less about his little brother at the moment. He'd just discovered a stash of mini-nuke proximity grenades. They'd be perfect when he attacked the stronghold at the end of the level.

Ten minutes later, Ruben started screaming. "Aliens! Help meeeee!!!!"

Henry heard footsteps race through the living room, along the hall, and into the kitchen. The back door slammed as Ruben ran into the yard. There was another scream, but Henry didn't pay any attention to it. His little brother was always screaming. Henry had more important things to deal with.

Finally, two hours later, Henry watched the credits scroll down the screen. "I did it." He'd beaten the game on his own, clearing the last five levels without any help from Stan.

Henry dropped the controller from his half-numb hands and staggered to his feet. His back ached from sitting in one spot for so long, and his legs tingled. He didn't care. He'd finished the game. That was the important thing. He needed to brag to someone about his accomplishment. Not just someone—he wanted to brag to everyone. But he'd start with the most convenient, and easily impressed, person.

"Hey, Ruben, where are you?"

No answer.

Henry walked out to the backyard. Instead of grass and a swing set, he found an enormous crater, like someone had set off a bomb. He went around the house to the front yard and looked down the street. Half the houses were on fire. A bunch of others were just gone, like a giant had scraped them up with a spatula.

Henry didn't see any people at all.

"Hey," he called, in case someone could hear him. "I beat *Alien Warfront.* All by myself. On the hard setting."

After a moment, Henry gave up and went back inside.

Might as well play another game, he thought. There was no point wasting the day. He called a couple of his friends, to see if anyone wanted to play online, but nobody answered.

So Henry played by himself and he was totally happy, until the electricity went off, the water stopped running, and the invaders made a second pass through town to wipe out any stragglers.

Despite all his gaming skills, Henry didn't turn out to be a very challenging opponent when he fought against real aliens. The battle was brief. And then it was GAME OVER forever.

GORGONZOLA

I watched the blood drain from Royce's face. His mouth dropped open like his jaw muscles had been slit. His eyes bulged as if someone had jammed high-pressure air hoses into both his ears and both his nostrils. He pointed a trembling finger at my parents' kitchen table.

"That's the most horrible thing I've ever seen. Or smelled." He clutched his nose and ran out of the kitchen.

I really couldn't argue. My folks ate some totally disgusting stuff. "Wait for me," I called.

"What was that?" Royce asked when I caught up with him in the living room.

"Gorgonzola," I said. "It's a kind of blue cheese."

"Man, it smells like someone blew it out their butt." He shook his head. "Who'd make something like that?"

I shrugged. "Not a clue."

But the question got me wondering. That night, after the cheese was safely wrapped up, I opened the fridge and looked at the label. GORGON FARMS GORGONZOLA. The address was on Millburg-Bayerton Road, the four-lane highway that, no surprise, ran between Millburg, where we lived, and Bayerton. I told Royce about it the next day in school.

"Hey, you know what a Gorgon is?" he said.

"Nope."

"That's like Medusa," he said.

This wasn't clearing things up at all. "Who?"

"Medusa. Don't you pay any attention in school?"

I shook my head. "I try not to."

"It's actually a cool story."

"And you're going to tell it to me, no matter what I say. Right?"

"Right."

I didn't try to fight it. Royce loved telling me stuff. So he told me about Medusa, who was so ugly that people who looked at her turned to stone. This guy named Perseus killed her by using his shield as a mirror. When she saw her own face, she turned to stone. Then Perseus cut off her head. I didn't bother asking Royce how you cut off a head when someone's turned to stone. Perseus must have had an awesome sword.

"We need to check this place out," he said.

"No, we don't. It's just some stupid farm. Probably a bunch of old hippies or something, living with cows or goats. Smelly people with smelly animals making smelly cheese. There's nothing to see."

"There must be," he said. "A cheese that horrible has to come from a horrifying cheesemaker. We're going there right after school."

I knew better than to argue. Once Royce decided to do something, it was easier to go along. So, after school, Royce and I caught the bus to Bayerton.

The whole way there, he kept touching his backpack, like he had something important inside.

"What's in there?" I asked.

"Nothing."

"It has to be something."

"I'll show you later."

I could tell he wasn't going to give me a real answer. I sat back until we got close to our stop. Finally, the bus pulled over to the side of the highway next to a small wooden sign for Gorgon Farms.

"This is such a total waste of time," I said as we got out.

"You have no sense of adventure," Royce said.

"Adventure isn't always a good thing." I looked past the sign. There was a gravel road curving out of sight beyond the trees.

Royce led the way. I followed him along the road, which ran through a dense forest of trees. Eventually, we reached a field.

"I told you there'd be goats," I said.

Sure enough, behind a fence, I saw goats and cows. Chickens, too. The cows were grazing near a barn. There was a brick building behind the barn that looked like a small factory.

"Let's check it out," Royce said.

We walked up to the building, then crouched on either side of a window.

"Someone's there," Royce whispered.

A woman, dressed in a long white robe that reminded me of a bedsheet, was in the room, with her back to us. She had thick, wavy hair that reached past her shoulders. A large cage on a table held three chickens. The woman reached into the cage, pulled out a chicken, and raised it up in both hands so it was level with her head.

The chicken jolted and jerked, like it had seen something startling. It let out a really pathetic squawk. And then it froze.

But that wasn't the weird part. It didn't just freeze. It changed color. The chicken wasn't brown and yellow anymore. It was white, with green and blue veins.

"Cheese!" Royce gasped. I slapped my hand over his mouth before he could say anything else. I didn't want the woman to hear us.

In the room, the woman took the cheese chicken to a table and started to cut it up into pieces. It wasn't bloody. There weren't any guts. The thing was solid cheese. Solid Gorgonzola.

I think guts would have been less disgusting.

The woman's hair wriggled and writhed. I realized it wasn't thick curls—it was thin snakes.

"We have to get out of here," I whispered.

"Not yet." Royce put his backpack down, unzipped it slowly enough that it didn't make much noise, and pulled out a mirror. It was about the size of a sheet of typing paper. "I borrowed this from the science room."

"Are you crazy?" I couldn't believe he was going to try to turn the Gorgon into stone. I mean, cheese.

"I have to see what happens." He held the mirror in front of his face, stood up, and shouted, "Hey! Look here!"

Not very subtle, but I guess it got her attention. I heard a pathetic squawk from inside.

Royce grinned at me. "I knew it would work." He tilted his head downward and raised the mirror a little bit. So he could see beneath it. I looked away, just in case.

"Cheese feet," Royce said. He raised the mirror higher. "Cheese legs."

He raised the mirror all the way. Then he let out a pathetic squawk and froze.

"Royce!"

I touched his arm. My fingers sank into something soft and creamy. It was solid Gorgonzola. I guess the Gorgon was still too horrifying to look at, even after she was turned to cheese. Maybe she was even more horrifying now.

As sad as it was to lose a friend, there wasn't any point sticking around. It's not like I could do anything for Royce.

I thought about breaking off a hunk of him for my parents, but that just seemed wrong, somehow.

It took a lot of willpower not to sneak a peek at the Gorgon for myself, but I managed to keep from turning my head toward a cheesy fate as I hurried away from the building.

I didn't relax until I got back to the highway. Then, without thinking, I licked my fingers.

Hmmm. Not bad. Kind of tangy and buttery. It tasted a lot better than it smelled. Actually, it tasted really good. I'd bet it would be great on crackers. But I was pretty sure it would never become my favorite cheese. Not now that I knew where it came from.

BLOWOUT

The moon was full, but despite its light, the stars were bright. Yes, it was poetic. But poetry wasn't on Arlen's mind. Power was on his mind. And his mind was full of power. From the time he'd first stared at the sky, he'd used his mind to tear apart clouds. He'd made leaves fall from trees, and icicles plunge from rooftop gutters. He'd once caused a bird to drop from the air, but that had seemed wrong, so he concentrated on things that didn't walk or crawl or swim or fly.

Now Arlen was ready for something grander than clouds or leaves. "Watch this," he told his sister Riva. "You'll be amazed." He aimed his finger at a star and blew out a sharp burst of air, as if he'd been struck full force in the stomach.

The star flickered faster than before, dimmed for a moment, then returned to normal.

"Cute," Riva said. "But not amazing."

"Wait," Arlen said before Riva could walk away. "I've almost got it."

He puffed again, changing the forces in subtle ways.

This time, the star vanished as if someone had splashed a blot of ink across it. The star itself, and all the light it cast, no longer existed.

"Gone," Arlen said. "Snuffed for good." He gave Riva a dark smile, then pointed toward another star, brighter than the first.

"Stop," Riva said. "You're always ruining things."

"There are countless stars," he said. "Nobody will miss this one."

He puffed it away.

"Or that one." He pointed toward the eastern horizon.

As he puffed, Riva put her hand in front of his mouth.

"Doesn't matter," Arlen said as the star vanished. "It's like an X-ray, or a powerful thought. Nothing can block it."

He walked over to a large maple tree on their front lawn, put his face an inch from the trunk, and puffed right through it, erasing another star.

"Stop it," Riva said. "Please."

Arlen laughed and faced the west, turning his back on Riva. "No. It makes me feel strong. I feel like I'll outlast the universe. Oh, there's a pretty one, all red and twinkly." He pointed toward the sky and drew in a breath.

"No!" Riva tackled him. He was older and taller, but Riva was motivated, and she understood leverage.

Arlen went down hard, with Riva's shoulder in his back. "*Oof!*" he puffed as his body struck the ground. The blast from his lips parted the grass.

Something changed.

Riva rolled off her brother, wondering why the stars were suddenly so much brighter and the world around her suddenly so much darker.

21

All was black except for the stars.

"The moon," Riva whispered. It was gone.

"How—?" Arlen said.

Riva pointed where the moon had been, all full and bright. "I don't know. You didn't aim that way."

Another thought hit her, striking with more force than a tackle. "The moon doesn't make its own light."

They looked down at the ground. Riva imagined the path of Arlen's power. It had shot through the earth, just as easily as it had passed through her hand or the tree. And it had struck a star on the other side. A star that warmed the earth and lit the moon.

Arlen had snuffed the sun.

The stars overhead twinkled in an endless night. On Earth, the air grew cold. Arlen outlasted the sun by several hours, but he didn't come close to outlasting the universe.

CHRISTMAS CAROL

Carol let out a small sigh of happiness as she sank back against the couch cushions and admired the wrapping paper scattered across the living room floor. Her parents had headed to the kitchen to whip up a strawberry-pancake breakfast. Her big brother had gone out to visit his friends. Her little brother had passed out on the floor—which wasn't a huge surprise, since he'd been awake half the night, too excited to sleep. He'd stumbled into her bedroom at least seven times to ask, "Is it Kwitsmats yet?" That was about as close as he could get to saying *Christmas*.

Ah, Christmas, Carol thought. That was the most wonderful word ever spoken.

"I wish every day was Christmas," she said aloud as she stroked the amazingly soft cashmere sweater her parents had given her. It had come with a matching scarf and gloves, just as gorgeous, and just as soft.

FWABOOMPH!

The glass doors in front of the fireplace flew open. Someone burst into the room. He was dressed like Santa Claus,

23

but in reverse, with a white outfit bordered in red trim. He was very thin, fairly young, and thoroughly sooty.

Carol didn't scream or jump or gasp. She went to school with the McGurdle triplets, who were totally hyperactive and always hurling things at one another, and with Valerie Tadzmire, who screamed at the top of her lungs every time she spotted a bug, or even a drawing of a bug. So Carol wasn't easily startled or disturbed.

"Is everything okay?" her mother called from the kitchen.

"It's just fine," Carol called back.

The stranger took a step toward her, then waited. Carol waited, too.

"Aren't you going to ask me who I am?" the stranger said.

"I'm pretty sure you're planning to tell me," Carol said.

"I am the Spirit of Christmas Presents," the stranger said, as if she had actually asked the question. "And I am here to grant you your wish."

"Wait," Carol said, holding up one hand. "A present and a wish aren't the same. You seem to be a bit mixed up. If you're the Spirit of Christmas Presents, why are you granting wishes? Shouldn't you be a genie or the Spirit of Christmas Wishes, or something like that, if you want to grant wishes?"

"Look, I don't make the rules," he said. He sneezed, then rubbed his soot-streaked nose with one hand.

"Ick. Cover your face next time," Carol said.

"Sorry." He took off his hat, wiped his nose, then put it back on. The hat, that is. The nose was already on.

"As I was saying, I have come here to grant you your wish and teach you a lesson. It will now always be Christmas. Every day. Forever." His voice deepened as he drew out the last word.

"Yay!" Carol said. "That's awesome. Every day?"

"Every single day," he said, as if this could possibly be a bad thing.

"Cool. Thanks." Carol slid off the couch and headed for the kitchen. It smelled like the pancakes were ready.

She spent a wonderful day enjoying her presents and exchanging messages with all her friends. None of them had gotten a cashmere sweater.

She was thrilled the next morning to discover that it was Christmas again. She got to unwrap a whole new pile of presents. Some were the same—her uncle Milton always sent her a calendar—but others were delightfully different. Instead of a sweater, she got two pairs of jeans and a belt.

And it was Christmas once again the morning after that. And the next morning. And the next.

Every day was Christmas.

After a month or two—Carol had stopped counting days—the fireplace doors FWABOOMPHed again, and the Spirit of Christmas Presents staggered out.

"Well, Carol," he said, "what have we learned?"

"Learned?" she asked.

He nodded. "Yes. What have we learned?"

"Well, there's no school on Christmas. So, while I can't speak for you, I know I've learned absolutely nothing." She held up a box of chocolates her aunt Gertrude had sent her. "Want one?" she asked.

"No, thank you. But listen—I'm not talking about things you learned, or didn't learn, in school. What has getting your wish taught you?"

Carol looked at the scattered presents, then sniffed the wonderful aroma of waffles, which her parents made on Christmas mornings when they didn't make pancakes, French toast, or coffee cake.

"Getting my wish has taught me that if you keep making impossible wishes, one of them might actually come true someday, and then things will be perfect and wonderful forever and ever."

"No, no, no," he said. "Aren't you tired of getting presents?"

"Are you kidding?" Carol reached down and picked up a doll from the pile of toys at her feet. "This one talks and takes videos. I got two new books, a microscope, and a beadcraft kit. If I wished for anything at all, it would be for a longer day."

"What about TV?" he asked. "Aren't you getting tired of the Christmas specials?"

Carol shook her head. "I could watch *A Christmas Story* all day, every day."

"No school?" he said.

"What's your point?" she asked.

The Spirit of Christmas Presents sighed, got up, and headed toward the fireplace. As he walked, he turned his coat inside out. Now it was orange and black.

"Where are you going?" Carol asked.

"There's a boy down the street who keeps wishing it would always be Halloween," he said.

"And now it's going to be?" Carol asked.

"For him, it will. Until he learns his lesson."

Carol thought about the kids in her neighborhood. "Is it Seth Porter?"

"That's the one." The Spirit of Christmas Presents took off his hat and turned it inside out, revealing more orange and black.

"He'll totally love it," she said. "He'll never want it to end."

"Great. Just great." The Spirit of Christmas Presents, who had now slipped into his Spirit of Halloween Treats outfit, climbed into the chimney.

Carol went back to examining the chocolates, trying to guess what was inside each one. It was wonderful knowing she didn't have to make them last. She'd get another box from one of her relatives next Christmas. And next Christmas was only a day away. A fabulous, present-filled, joy-strewn day.

She nibbled the corner of one of the chocolates. "Mm-mmm, lemon creme."

A moment later, from halfway up the chimney, she heard a faint voice call, "Just give a shout if you ever realize how dreadful and meaningless your life has become."

"I'll do that," Carol said. But she knew she never would.

THRESHOLDS OF PAIN

I t was our last night at the beach. We'd been there a week, and had gotten wonderfully burned by the sun, beaten by the surf, and abraded by the sand. We'd already explored all of Wavecrest Cove, the town where we were staying, so after dinner, Dad drove us down to Regence Beach, which had a short boardwalk and an amusement pier.

There was only one roller coaster, but it was a good one. Dad and I rode it twice, once up front, and once in the back car, while Mom took my little brother and sister on the kiddie rides.

We played some games after that, even though Dad told us there wasn't much chance of winning. He was right, but it was still fun to try.

Then I saw it. Right between the BB gun shooting gallery and what must have been the eighty-seventh pizza place. BUCK NORDSTRUM'S AUTHENTIC AMAZING SIDESHOW. That's what the sign said.

"Dad, look!" I grabbed his arm and pointed at the posters

over the entrance. They promised wonders beyond anything the human mind could imagine.

I saw Dad's expression. He was interested, even though the interest was quickly replaced by a good-parent face. "That's not really appropriate entertainment for young people," he said.

"Oh, come on. There's a guy who eats glass! And a lady who turns into a gorilla! We have to go. There's no way we can miss this."

I watched Mom to see whether she'd have a problem with it. If she didn't kill the idea, I knew I could get Dad to go.

She barely frowned. "I'll never understand why you're so fascinated by that sort of thing."

That was good enough to make me forge ahead. "Please, Dad? There's nothing like this anywhere near us. It's our only chance. Remember when we went to the Ripley's Museum in San Francisco? That was awesome. This will be great, too. Can we?"

I totally loved anything weird—monsters, carnivals, flying saucers, aliens with three eyes and tentacles.

"I guess. . . ."

Score. I tried to keep from bouncing off the boardwalk while Dad bought two tickets. I followed him inside to the waiting area. According to the sign, the next show started in ten minutes.

"Ever been to a sideshow?" I asked.

"Once, back when I was your age," he said.

"Was it good?"

"As far as I remember." The corner of his mouth twitched into an odd little smirk when he said that.

"What?"

"This one guy hammered a nail up his nose." Dad held his hand up, with his first finger and thumb spread all the way out. "It was this big."

"You're kidding." I tried to imagine that.

"Nope, I'm not kidding. I'll never forget it."

A curtain opened at the far end of the room. A man dressed in a white shirt with a black vest came out and walked to the front of a small stage.

"Welcome. I am Buck Nordstrum. Prepare to be thrilled, dazzled, terrified, and amazed beyond your wildest dreams."

The first act was a fire-eater. "Pretty cool," I whispered to Dad as the man put flaming torches in his mouth. We were so close, I could feel the heat. There were only about a dozen other people watching the show, so it was easy to get a spot right near the action.

Dad gave me a funny look. I realized *cool* wasn't the best description. But the act was definitely amazing. I'd seen fire-eaters on TV, but never in person.

When the fire-eater was finished, a woman came onto the stage and did a sword-swallowing act. Then they rolled out a chair with the headless lady. I was pretty sure that was a trick. Actually, I was positive it was a trick. Still, it was fun to see. I don't mind being tricked.

There were six more acts, including the lady who turned into a gorilla—which was definitely a trick, and probably the same performer who'd lost her head earlier—and then Buck Nordstrum stepped back onstage.

"Ladies and gentlemen . . ." He nodded in my direction and added, "And young men, too. We come to the final act. I present to you—myself. Buck Nordstrum, the Invulnerable Man."

As he removed his vest, I wondered what sort of trick this would involve. He unbuttoned his shirt, took it off, folded it, and placed it over the back of a chair, on top of the vest. Then he reached into a leather bag at his feet—like the kind of bag doctors carry—and removed a metal knitting needle.

"I must warn you—my performance might be too disturbing for sensitive individuals. If you need to leave, the exit is over there." He pointed toward a door to our right. An exit sign flickered briefly, then went dark again.

"You okay?" Dad asked.

"Sure. Are you?"

"Can't be any worse than the nail up the nose."

Buck Nordstrum pushed the knitting needle into his left forearm, midway between his wrist and elbow. It pierced the top of his arm. He pushed the needle deeper. The skin on the back of his arm bulged. Half a heartbeat later, the point of the knitting needle burst through. He held up his arm and rotated it, so we could see it—and the needle—from all sides. After a moment, he eased the needle back out.

There was no blood. Based on his expression, it didn't look like there was any pain, either.

I shuddered and moved a step closer to Dad.

"Want to leave?" he asked.

I thought about it. This was the last act, so I wouldn't miss much if we left. I wasn't sure whether I wanted to find out what Buck Nordstrum would do next. But when he pulled the long knife from his bag and placed the point of the blade against his throat, I knew I had to stay.

As the blade sank in, half the people rushed for the exit. It sounded like one person threw up, but I couldn't take my eyes off the stage. Dad put a hand on my shoulder. "I've seen enough."

He stepped toward the exit. I didn't follow, but I glanced in his direction. Dad turned back. "Come on."

"Can I stay?"

His gaze moved from me to the stage, and then back. Buck had turned sideways, so everyone could see the knife trying to break through the skin at the back of his neck. "You sure?"

"I've seen worse things in video games," I said. "And on the news."

That was true. I'd blown alien heads right off with sniper rifles, and ripped limbs from six-armed foes. Violence on the TV wasn't real to me. They were always showing people getting hurt on the news.

This performance was real, and kind of scary, but I wasn't going to admit it to Dad, and I wasn't going to miss out on seeing whatever Buck Nordstrum was going to do next.

"Okay. I trust you to know what you can handle. I'll meet you right outside."

By the time Dad reached the door, the knife was jutting out the back of Buck Nordstrum's neck.

I thought he'd just yank it free. But he shifted his grip on the hilt and pulled the handle toward the left side of his neck. The point moved toward the right side. After slicing a quarter way around, he pulled the blade out.

As hard as I stared, I couldn't see any sort of cut in his neck. His flesh flowed like rubber around the blade. It had to be a trick. But how could it be? There was nothing between him and the knife except for bare skin. No tubes, no boxes, no silk scarves, none of the stuff magicians use to hide how their tricks work.

The next sharp point—this time in the form of a railroad spike—went into his stomach. By then, there were only two other people left in the audience.

They cleared out when it became obvious that Buck Nordstrum's final stunt involved a pair of scissors and his right eye.

I stayed.

After he pulled out the scissors, he bowed. "Show's over, kid."

I wasn't ready to leave. There was something I had to know. And it wasn't about how he did his act. I was pretty sure I'd figured out his secret.

"How long have you been here?" I asked.

"Five years." He put the scissors down on the table. "We opened the show right after they extended the boardwalk."

"Not *here*," I said, pointing to the stage. "I mean, here on Earth."

He turned away from me and started putting things back in his bag. "I don't know what you're talking about."

"Yeah, you do. You aren't human. Which means you're either a monster or an alien."

That got his attention. He locked his eyes—both of which were totally undamaged—on mine. "If I'm a monster, you're better off not being alone with me. Monsters eat small boys."

I shivered. But I stood my ground. "I'm not small. And I don't believe in monsters." I pointed up toward the ceiling, and past it to the stars. "But I do believe in life on other planets."

He didn't say anything.

"I'm guessing you're stuck here." That was the only possible explanation I could think of for him to start a business on the boardwalk. Even aliens need food and shelter. "So, how long?"

"Fifty years."

I hadn't expected him to admit it, and I really hadn't expected he'd been here that long. I studied his face as he put his shirt back on. He didn't look any older than my dad. But he could shove a large needle through his flesh without bleeding, and he healed instantly. I guess if he said he'd been here for five hundred years, I'd have to believe him.

I looked toward the exit. Dad wouldn't wait much longer before checking on me. But there was one more thing I wanted to know.

"Are you stuck here?" I asked.

"For now," he said. "My people might come by again in fifty or a hundred years."

"You must feel really homesick." I couldn't imagine being stranded an another planet, far away from everything I grew up with. "Don't you miss your friends and family?"

He picked up the knife.

I took a step back, but I relaxed when I realized he wasn't coming after me.

"Miss them?" He pressed the point of the blade against his palm until it pierced the flesh. "No more than I feel this."

That's when I realized how truly alien he was. And how alien I must be to him. All of us on Earth must seem alien, for that matter, with our feelings, our emotions, our pain. As I backed toward the door, I knew I needed to say something more.

"I liked the show," I said. The words felt weak and stupid.

But they made him smile. "Thank you. That's good to hear."

I stepped outside, back into the normal oddness of the boardwalk. As I left the sideshow behind, I couldn't help scanning the sky, drinking in the awesomeness of the universe.

Dad was waiting for me on a bench by the railing. I saw Mom and the rest of my family in line at a frozen custard stand.

"Did it get much worse?" Dad asked when I joined him.

"A lot worse," I said. "The ending was terrible. But I'm glad I stayed."

SMART FOOD

I was heading out to my friend Sally's house when I heard a whisper.

"Hey, kid . . ."

I looked around. There was nobody in sight.

"Pssst. Down here."

I looked down. I was standing near Mom's vegetable garden. There wasn't anybody in the garden, either. It would be pretty tough to hide behind a head of lettuce or even an overgrown oregano bush.

"Right here!"

The voice was louder. And, now that I was looking at the garden, I could actually tell where it came from. But it couldn't be coming from where it came from. No way.

"You do hear me, don't you?"

"Uh, yeah . . ." I couldn't believe I was talking to a clump of broccoli. Before I said anything else, I checked to make sure nobody saw me. It wouldn't be good to get a reputation for holding conversations with vegetables. "I definitely hear you."

"Good. Because we have a lot to talk about."

I dropped to my knees so I could get a closer look. As far as I could see, it was just a regular clump of broccoli. "Where's your mouth?"

"I don't have one. There's more than one way to make sound."

"And how can you talk at all? You're a vegetable. You don't even have a brain."

"I don't have a meat brain, like yours. But I can think. All of us can think. But I'm the first one who can communicate with people. I don't know why. It's just the way I was sprouted. My people have been trying to get in touch with your people for centuries."

"You're telling me that all vegetables can think?"

"We can think quite clearly," the broccoli said. "And feel. We're quite sensitive. Considering what happens to most of us, that's not a good thing."

"Ouch. You really can feel?" I pictured carrots being peeled and diced, and asparagus being battered and dropped into boiling oil. I shuddered at the image. But at the same time, my mouth watered at the memory of that crispy, tender asparagus. My folks had ordered it once when we'd had dinner at a fancy steak house. It tasted amazing.

"Yes. We can feel. That's why I needed to get your attention. You must tell the rest of the humans to stop cooking us and eating us. It's just not right."

"But then we'd starve," I said.

"You can eat animals. There are plenty to chose from—mammals, birds, fish."

"But don't they think and have feelings, too?" I'd always hoped that animals didn't have the same kind of feelings as humans, but I was pretty sure they had some kind of feelings.

"No way," the broccoli said. "Animals are the real vegetables. No thoughts. Nothing going on between the ears. They're really just animated meals. Think of them as movable feasts."

I thought about animals. They were cute. If people didn't eat any vegetables, they'd eat a lot more animals. I didn't want to eat nothing but meat. I like lettuce on my hamburgers. I didn't want to eat nothing but vegetables, either. I couldn't imagine the Fourth of July without hot dogs on the grill. I liked both.

"Well," the broccoli said as I tried to figure out how to deal with the situation, "are you going to do something about this, or do I have to talk with someone else?"

"No need. I'll do something." I leaned over and grabbed the broccoli with both hands. The scream it let out when I yanked it from the ground wasn't pleasant. Luckily, the scream quickly faded to a whimper, and soon after that, slipped into silence. By the time I reached Sally's house, the clump of broccoli was just another voiceless vegetable.

Now I had to figure out what to do with it. There was no way I could throw it out. That would have been wasteful and wrong. The world's first talking vegetable deserved more respect than that. But I really didn't want to eat it myself—not after we'd had that conversation. I'd hear its voice with every bite. The answer was right in front of me.

"I brought you something from my mom's garden," I told Sally when she answered the door. "I just picked it."

"Thanks! It looks delicious." She took the broccoli from me. "Maybe you can stay for dinner. My dad is grilling steaks."

"That sounds great," I said, "but I don't think I'll be hungry for a while. I just had my fill of vegetables."

THE ART OF ALCHEMY

Come closer. . . ."

The voice was a croaking gasp. Lenny hesitated. His great-grandfather was scary enough normally. But now, lying on the hospital bed, the old man looked like he'd already died. Lenny glanced over his shoulder. His parents had gone to the cafeteria. He was alone.

"Now!"

The old man shuddered like the shout had taken all his strength. Lenny shuffled forward, wishing he were home or even at school. Anywhere but here.

"I spent half my life seeking the secret of modern alchemy," the old man said. He raised his head and repeated the last two words as if they were a magical phrase: *modern alchemy*.

Lenny tried to pretend he was paying attention. He'd only met his great-grandfather a couple times.

"I found it last month."

I don't care, Lenny thought. He had no idea what the old man was babbling about.

"Riches," the old man said. "Unbelievable wealth."

Lenny started to pay attention.

"It should have been mine. Vast and endless wealth. It's too late for me. Take it for yourself."

"Take what?" Lenny asked.

"The secret. It's all written down." The old man told Lenny where to find the notebook. Then he died.

After the funeral, when his parents were cleaning out his great-grandfather's house, Lenny pried up the loose board in the attic floor and removed the small notebook. He didn't even look at it until he was alone in his bedroom that evening.

The pages were filled with diagrams and formulas. None of it made any sense to Lenny. But science wasn't his best subject. Neither was math. Or English.

As much as he wanted to be rich, he knew this could all be a waste of time. But the next day, right before school started, he hunted down Marvin Wetburg, the smartest kid in his class.

All of Marvin's nerd friends scattered when Lenny walked over. Marvin held up his Yoda lunch box in a shaking hand and said, "Here. I don't have any money. But you can have my sandwich. It's free-range chicken on whole wheat with alfalfa sprouts. And chocolate-macadamia cookies."

"I don't want your sandwich," Lenny said. But he did like the way Marvin trembled. It was nice being powerful. "I want to know something."

Marvin lowered Yoda. "What?"

"There's a word. . . ." Lenny paused. He realized he hadn't written down the word, and it wasn't on the notebook.

"I'm good with words," Marvin said. His trembles had calmed from violent shakes to random twitches, but it was pretty likely his chocolate-macadamia cookies were no longer intact.

"It's for getting rich," Lenny said. "Alka-something."

Marvin scrunched his forehead. Then his eyes widened. "Alchemy?"

"Yeah," Lenny said, remembering those awful moments in the hospital. "That's the word. What's it mean?"

"Lots of things," Marvin said. "The alchemists searched for the homunculus, for example. And they explored—"

Lenny clamped a hand on Marvin's shoulder. Big words made him want to hit things. "Can alchemy make you rich?"

Marvin nodded. It looked like he was trying to talk. Lenny let go of his shoulder.

"Yeah, it can make you rich," Marvin said. "If it were real. The alchemists wanted to turn lead into gold. Lead is really inexpensive. Gold is really valuable. Anyone who could turn lead to gold would be insanely rich."

Insanely rich. "Meet me after school," Lenny said.

"Can't you just hit me now and get it over with?" Marvin asked. "Anticipation is torture."

"I'm not going to hit you," Lenny said. "At least, not if you do what I tell you."

Lenny had a hard time keeping his mind on his lessons that day. None of his teachers noticed, since that wasn't any different from his usual behavior in class.

After school, Lenny brought Marvin home and showed him the notebook. "Can you build this?" he asked.

Marvin started to thumb through the pages. It took a long time. Lenny wanted to shake him, but he figured that would just slow things down. Shaking Marvin would be like rebooting a computer over and over.

Finally, Marvin closed the notebook and said, "I can make this. I actually have most of the parts."

"How long will it take?" Lenny asked. He was eager to get rich.

"A week. There's a lot of wiring to deal with. It should be finished by Saturday."

"Great." Lenny knew the perfect place to go. There was an old lead mine on the other side of the county park. His class had visited the place on a field trip. The teacher had told them there was still plenty of lead left in the mine, but it wasn't worth the effort to dig it out. Soon, all that lead would be gold, and it would all be his.

On Saturday, Lenny met up with Marvin by the park. Marvin had a red wagon with a large piece of plywood in it. A bird's nest of red and blue wires sat on top of the wood, connecting dozens of small electronic parts, several dials, a clump of steel wool, a flask of clear liquid, and one large battery that looked like it had been borrowed from a riding mower.

"That's it?" Lenny asked.

"Yeah. I made it exactly like the diagrams. I couldn't test it. It's still stabilizing, but it should be ready to use by the time we get to the mine. I really don't understand how it works, though it definitely performs a transmutation."

Lenny clenched his fists. "Transmu . . ."

"Never mind." Marvin headed across the park.

The path that led to the mine was blocked, but every kid in town knew how to get through it. Lenny carried the machine when the ground got too rough for the wagon. It was heavy, but he was strong.

"Uh-oh," Marvin said when they reached the entrance to the tunnel. "It's kind of wet." He tapped his foot at the edge of a puddle. There was water all over the floor. "And it's dark. I won't be able to see what I'm doing. Maybe we'd better leave."

"No way. I'll build a fire." Lenny liked fires. And there was plenty of wood right outside. In a couple minutes, he had a fire going, twenty feet from the entrance, where nobody would see the smoke. It didn't do much for the damp floor, but it warmed the damp, chilly air. "Okay. It's time to get rich." He turned toward the nearest wall. "Which part is the lead?"

"There's no free lead in a mine," Marvin said.

"I have to pay for it?" Lenny asked.

"No. Don't be stu—" Marvin choked off the insult and took a hard swallow before speaking again. "My mistake. I didn't explain it right. The lead is mixed up with other elements and minerals. But once it becomes gold, we can extract it easily enough. Any of that shiny ore would work fine. That's galena."

Lenny pulled a hammer and chisel from his backpack and whacked off a hunk of rock from the wall. He smiled as he imagined the heavy hunk of metal turning into gold.

"How's this?"

"That's a good start," Marvin said. He hooked a pair of wires to the piece of rock. Then he rested his finger against a button on the side of the machine. "Ready?"

"I'll do it," Lenny said.

"Fine." Marvin stepped away from the machine.

As Lenny reached for the button, he thought about his great-grandfather, and about the spark of excitement that had allowed the old man to raise his head from his pillows. "Modern alchemy." Lenny repeated the words he'd heard in the hospital. Then he pushed the button. The machine hummed.

"What did you say?" Marvin asked.

"Modern alchemy," Lenny said. "That's what this is."

The nerd's body jerked like he was the one connected to the battery. "You idiot!" He turned and raced for the exit.

Lenny froze, his attention shifting from Marvin's back to the lump of rock that would become gold very soon. Nobody called him names. Not ever. He was going to pound the nerd. But he was going to make a ton of gold first.

Marvin was almost at the exit. He spun back toward Lenny. "Run! Hurry! You're gonna get hurt!"

For the first time in ages, Lenny had a complex thought. He realized what was happening. The nerd was trying to trick him into leaving so he could keep all the gold for himself. But Lenny wasn't going to fall for it. How awesome was that? He'd outsmarted a nerd.

Marvin was still shouting stuff. "I didn't know it was *modern* alchemy," he said. "That's different. Alchemy—the ancient kind—is turning lead to gold. Modern alchemy is turning water to gasoline. I tried to warn you." He spun away and dashed out of the tunnel.

Water to gasoline?

Lenny looked down. The hunk of rock attached to the wires was still dull and worthless. But the water around it shimmered with rainbow flashes. The shimmer spread, reflecting the light of the fire. All the water on the cave floor changed. The air filled with the smell of gasoline.

Too late, Lenny decided to run for the exit.

There was a *whumpf*, followed by an agonizing wave of heat as the gasoline vapors exploded.

Marvin, who'd reached the exit, was knocked twenty feet through the air, but he landed in a bed of leaves and escaped without anything more than some major bruises.

Lenny, on the other hand, was toast.

MAGNIFYING
THE TRAGEDY

Colton and Ozzie took a break from reading horror comics to go outside and fry some ants with Colton's new magnifying glass. The magnifying glass was one sixteenth of the Super Science Sleuth Sixteen-in-One Amazing Pocket Tool that Colton's mother had bought for him in an attempt to get him interested in something useful.

"Awesome!" Ozzie shouted as he turned an innocent insect into a small, crunchy clump of carbon.

"My turn." Colton snatched the magnifying glass out of Ozzie's sweaty hand. The tool also had a tiny telescope, a microscope, a mirror for flashing secret messages to other super scientists, and a dozen other devices that were, for the most part, incapable of ruining the lives of insects in cruel and creative ways.

Neither of the boys paid any attention to the jet plane that cruised across the sky, thirty-six thousand feet above them, though either the telescope or binoculars would have given them a good look at it.

As Colton went to work lowering the local ant population, Ozzie glanced around nervously. "You know what?" he said.

"What?" Colton asked.

"If this were a horror story, we'd be in big trouble," Ozzie said.

"Yeah." Colton moved the magnifying glass over his next victim. "Good thing it isn't."

Ozzie nodded. "Real good thing. 'Cause if this were a horror story, you know what would happen, right?"

"Yeah, I know," Colton said as he fried another ant. "Somehow, we'd end up getting fried ourselves. An evil giant would pop up with a magnifying glass, or some space telescope would spin the wrong way and zap us with sunlight. Stuff like that is always happening in horror stories."

Ozzie reached for the magnifying glass. "Let me have it."

"Not yet." Colton pulled his hand back. The tool wriggled, flashing sunlight off the mirror.

Far above, the pilot of the jet plane noticed the flash. Briefly distracted from his duties, he bumped the landing-gear switch. He quickly corrected his error. But the stress caused a small piece of metal in the underbelly of the plane, which had already been weakened, to break apart.

Ozzie glanced all around. "No sign of anything that could fry us," he said. "Guess we can keep going."

"Guess so," Colton said. "I'm glad we aren't in a horror story."

"My turn." Ozzie made another grab for the magnifying glass. This time, he was successful. He heard the distant roar of jet engines, but didn't even bother to look up.

As the metal piece broke from the underbelly of the plane,

a flap opened near the tail section. Fifty gallons of blue liquid from the holding tank of the jet's toilet spilled out, instantly freezing in the biting cold of the upper atmosphere.

The frozen block of sludge, pulled by gravity and flung by the momentum of the plane, plummeted toward the ground in a perfect trajectory for a close encounter with two boys and sixteen tools.

"Huh?" Ozzie said as a shadow fell across the lens of the magnifying glass. He glanced up just in time to see that there was no fire involved in his inescapable and immediate doom. No sunlight. No evil giant with a magnifying glass. No out-of-control space telescope. There was just a rock-hard chunk of really gross blue ice about to smack into him and Colton at high speed, and crush them like bugs.

Some ants died, too. But the rest of them, those outside the range of the impact crater, were left in peace.

SWEET DREAMS

It's really not a good idea to annoy a witch.

We didn't mean to. All Stacy and I wanted to do was peek into the old woman's house and catch her doing something witchy, like putting bat wings into a kettle or turning her cat into a person.

Instead, we got caught.

We must have jumped at least three feet in the air when the witch's door flew open. I wanted to run, but I was too scared to move.

"Ah, what do we have here?" she said. "Two lovely young ladies decided to pay me a visit. What a pleasant surprise. Come in."

"Uh, we can't," I said.

"Have to get home," Stacy said.

"Well, it would be rude of me to let you leave without gifts." The witch reached into the side pockets of her skirt and pulled out two small paper bags. She thrust one at me. I grabbed it. It felt like a sack of pebbles. Stacy took the other bag.

"What is it?" I asked.

"Candy," the witch said. "Simply irresistible candy."

I peeked inside. The bag was filled with jelly beans. Mixed aromas of fruit, honey, and spices teased my nose.

"Go on," the witch said. "Run off. Scat."

We scampered off the porch. As we reached the sidewalk, the witch called after us, "Oh, one more thing. Whoever finishes her bag first will die." She let out a cackle that scratched down my spine like a razor-sharp fingernail.

I skidded to a halt and spun around, not believing I'd heard her right. "Die?" I asked.

She smiled even wider and nodded. "Die. *D-i-e.* So eat slowly."

Stacy let out a whimper and raced away. I followed her. As soon as we turned the corner, she said, "I'm getting rid of mine." She tossed her bag on the ground.

I threw mine down, too. I knew littering was bad, but dying struck me as worse.

"Let's get out of here," Stacy said.

"Yeah. Good idea."

But as we walked down the street, it felt like my guts were attached to the bag by a fishhook on a rubber band. I tried to keep going, but after two blocks the pain was so bad, I almost fell to my knees. I clutched my stomach and moaned. Stacy moaned, too.

I staggered backward. The pain faded a bit.

I took a couple more steps toward the bags.

The pain was definitely going away. To test it, I moved toward Stacy. The pain grew worse.

"We can't leave the bags," I said. "I'll get them."

I grabbed the bags and did something I'm not at all proud

of. I gave Stacy my bag. There was no way she could tell. They looked the same.

I didn't want to die. And I remembered the witch's words. Not just the ones promising us that whoever ate her candy first would die. But the other part. Those two words: *irresistible candy*.

"Nothing is really irresistible," Stacy said. "We can be strong."

"I hope so." I peeked into the bag. Even now, the sweet smell was tickling my tongue. The craving was worse than the pain. I'd have to eat a piece soon. But I'd eat Stacy's candy, not mine. That might seem terrible, but if one of us was going to die, why should it be me?

We reached my house. I dropped down on the porch steps and tried to calm myself. "Wow, that was weird." I put the bag by my feet.

"Yeah, totally weird," Stacy said. "You really think we could die?"

"No way," I said. "She was just trying to scare us. Right?"

"Yeah, you have to be right. Nobody is that mean." She sighed. Then she hiccuped.

"Take a deep breath," I said.

She tried that. It didn't help. "I always hiccup when I get real scared. This is awful." She slumped down and wrapped her arms around her head, like she wanted to disappear into a tight ball of flesh. Her body jerked with each hiccup. They seemed to be growing stronger.

"I'll get you some water." I ran in, filled a glass, and brought it back to the porch. Even on the short trip to the kitchen, I could feel my stomach start to hurt. I rushed back with the water I had to poke Stacy on the shoulder to get her to uncurl enough to take the glass. I was glad I got it for her. I felt especially sorry for her since she was going to die.

We talked for a while, until Stacy felt calm enough to walk home. I held my breath as she stepped away, hoping my stomach wouldn't hurt when she took my candy with her. Then she'd know I'd tricked her, and she'd take her own bag back. But I was fine.

After she left, I tasted the jelly beans. They were beyond delicious. Each one I ate made me crave more. Before I knew it, I'd eaten half the bag. I needed to slow down. I hadn't meant for Stacy to die right away.

A shiver ran through me as I thought about that. She wasn't as strong as I was. If she'd tasted the jelly beans, she could be gobbling up the whole bag right now. I could be close to death!

I opened the bag, scooped up a handful of the jelly beans, and started gobbling them down. My mouth filled with a brilliantly amazing mix of fresh strawberries, chocolate, cinnamon, and an endless, shifting swirl of other flavors. Soon, the bag was empty and I had the last jelly bean in my hand.

Stacy was about to die. We'd been friends forever. I had to admit feeling a ton of guilt. But not enough to keep me from popping the final jelly bean into my mouth. I bit down on it. Another burst of amazing flavor filled my mouth.

"Wait!"

I looked up as I heard the shout. Stacy was running back toward my house.

I put the empty bag behind my back. "What's wrong?" A ripple of fear shot through me at the thought that my trick had been discovered, but there was no way she could have figured out what I'd done.

"I'm a terrible friend," she said.

"You're a great friend." I rolled the bitten pieces of the jelly bean between my tongue and the roof of my mouth. I really didn't want to see Stacy die right in front of me. I wondered whether she'd just flop over, or wither up in some horrible, witchy ending. Either way, I'd rather not see it happen.

"No, I'm not a great friend. I'm terrible." She sobbed and held up her bag, which still looked full. "This is yours."

"What are you talking about?"

"I switched them," she said. "When you went for the water."

I gasped. Something got stuck in my throat.

Stacy kept talking. "I took your bag so I could eat all your candy. I didn't want to die. But I realized I couldn't do something so mean and evil to my best friend in the whole world. Maybe neither of us has to die. Maybe we could help each other resist the candy. Do you think that would work? I haven't even eaten a single one yet. Well, maybe one or two. But not a whole lot. I know I can resist them."

I tried to answer her, but my throat had closed up. The last piece of jelly bean felt like it was swelling. I waved my hand for help, but Stacy was so busy getting rid of her guilt, she didn't seem to notice that I was choking. She just kept talking.

"Can you ever forgive me? I know I was rotten. But I came back and confessed right away. So there wasn't any real harm. Please, say you forgive me."

I wanted to point at my throat, but I was too weak to lift my arms.

"Okay, I understand," Stacy said. "You're too angry to talk to me right now. That's okay. I'll come back later. But I promise, I won't eat any more of your jelly beans. I'll take really good care of them."

Stacy walked away.

The taste in my mouth, the amazing taste of irresistible candy, faded away, along with everything else.

CHIPMUNKS OFF
THE OLD BLOCK

I used to love watching chipmunks. I stopped loving it five or six minutes ago. That's when the drama I was watching ended. The whole thing, from start to finish, didn't take much longer than that.

I was in my backyard. We had a bench under the willow tree. I like to sit there and read, or just watch the squirrels and chipmunks. There are hawks around here, too. And once in a while, I'll spot a woodchuck or a rabbit. I saw a hawk catch a mouse once. That was pretty awesome, although I don't think the mouse shared my enjoyment.

We're not totally in the country, but there's a lot of unde-veloped land around here, so the animals have plenty of room to live. You don't have to travel too far to see deer, or even a family of foxes. But chipmunks were the best.

I was watching two chipmunks play some sort of game. One would chase the other. In the middle of a mad dash, they'd switch roles. And then they'd both skitter around like they were trying to catch an invisible friend. They acted pretty much like cartoon characters, except they didn't hit each other with frying pans or toss dynamite at the neighbor's dog. Though they did crash into things once in a while. I couldn't believe how silly they were.

I guess I was watching them too closely, since I didn't notice the spaceship at first. It wasn't so large that it blotted out the sun. It was around the size of a small bus. Though buses aren't shaped like two fighter jets jammed tail to tail. And they aren't made of shiny red metal. It moved silently, which is why I didn't hear it right away, either.

I definitely noticed the spaceship when it landed about ten feet to my left. A hatch opened on top, and two aliens came out. They were about three feet tall, with smooth orange skin and faces like jackals. But friendly jackals.

They had something in their hands. It looked like a bullhorn on a microphone stand. The large end was pointed upward, and the small part was attached to the stand. They jammed the stand into the ground. Then one of them flipped a switch.

The alien spoke. It was a weird sound, like how you'd sing if your tongue were made of sandpaper and your mouth were made of cement. Which is still better than I sound when I sing.

Somehow, real words came out of the cone. I guess it was a translator.

"We need help."

The other alien spoke. "We seek your most intelligent life-form."

Cool. I wondered what they needed. I could tell them where to find water. Or how to get in touch with the police. I knew all the local gas stations, too, though I figured the spaceship used some other kind of fuel.

"What do you need?" I asked. I was already picturing myself on the news, or maybe even shaking hands with the president.

A bird swooped past the cone and chirped. Words came out.

"Worms. Looking for worms. Have you seen worms?"

The dog next door barked. The cone translated. "Tommy will be home soon. I love Tommy. Tommy will be home soon. Tommy is my friend. Tommy loves me."

My cat peered out through the screen in my bedroom window, meowing. "Nap time."

Two chipmunks dashed up to the cone. They started chittering. A flurry of words came out. I smiled as I tried to guess what they'd say.

"Trajectory, rotation, beryllium, tangent course to the apogee . . ."

"Conservation of momentum, fractal solutions, ontogeny."

"Third derivative."

"Under the asymptote."

One of the aliens leaned toward them and screamed, "Focus!"

Both chipmunks stopped chittering and stood straight up on their hind legs, staring at the aliens.

"Our inertial guidance system has malfunctioned," the other alien said. "We believe it is a software issue. But neither of us is sufficiently trained in these things to fix the error."

"Got it!" one of the chipmunks said.

They started chittering at each other again as they raced onto the ship. I heard some clanks and then, I swear, a typing sound.

"They have such a hard time staying on task," one alien said.

"That's just because they're so brilliant," the other said. "I can't imagine being that smart. It must be difficult."

"It must."

"I'm glad we managed to get them to focus on our problem."

A moment later, the chipmunks dashed off the ship.

"All fixed," one of them said.

"Molybdenum would have made a better hull," the other said.

"Consider the malleability," the first one said, and they were off, spewing more words, like a couple physicists trying to rap.

I waved to get the aliens' attention. "I'm pretty smart, too. I got a B-plus on my last math test. Can I see your ship?"

They ignored me and went back through the hatch. I watched them leave. And then I tried to watch the chipmunks as they skittered and frolicked around my yard. But it just wasn't the same anymore. Nothing was.

*J*TUCK UP

I got it!" **Gilbert** shouted as he hustled to his right to snag the line drive. It looked like a tough catch. He knew he'd have to leap if he wanted a chance to stop the ball.

Around the field, he heard shouts and cheers. He also heard Damon yell, "I got it!" But the words didn't sink in. Not right away. Definitely not in time to avoid a collision.

Gilbert figured it all out as he tumbled to the ground after he and Damon crashed together beneath the hissing ball.

For a moment, Gilbert sat where he'd landed, wondering whether he'd broken anything. He heard the distant smack of a ball into a glove. Someone had fielded the drive and thrown it to first.

"You okay?" Damon asked.

Gilbert looked up at his friend, who had already gotten to his feet. "I think so." As he spoke, he realized that something was different. He probed his mouth with his tongue. Not different—missing.

"Oh, no. . . ." Gilbert raised a hand to his lips.

"What's wrong?" Damon asked. "You chip a tooth?"

"No. I think I swallowed my gum." Gilbert scanned the ground all around the spot where he'd landed, hoping to see a large wad of pink Mega-Chew Bubble Gum.

There was no sign of it.

He swallowed, trying to feel whether anything was stuck in his throat. It was hard to tell for sure.

"Really?" Damon asked. "You gulped your gum?"

"Yeah." Gilbert put a hand against his chest. "I wonder how far down it is." He tried to sense the location of the gum. Was it in his stomach already?

"Oh, man," Damon said. "It's going to gum you up."

"No, it won't," Gilbert said. But in his mind, he pictured a stomach full of gears and wheels clogged with gum. Big wads of pink gum stretched between the teeth of the gears. The parts tried to turn, but they couldn't. Everything was clogged.

"Yes, it will," Damon said. "I heard about a kid over in Falworth who swallowed his gum and they had to give him an operation."

"That's stupid," Gilbert said. "If gum was that dangerous, they wouldn't sell it to kids."

As Gilbert spoke, Terry Mackenzie went flying past the ball field on his skateboard. Across the park, Gilbert could see a kid trying to ride his bike while sitting backward on the seat. In a field on the other side of the road, a couple of kids were launching model rockets.

"I don't know," Damon said. "We can buy all sorts of dangerous stuff."

Gilbert stood up. He moved slowly, still making sure he hadn't been hurt. Everything seemed fine. But his stomach felt sort of tight, the way it got when he worried about something like a math test or a shot from the doctor.

"Are you going to keep playing?" Damon asked.

"Yeah," Gilbert said. "No reason not to." He walked back to his position at second base.

The game went on.

Gilbert made sure there was no chance of crashing when he dived for another line drive. This one wasn't anywhere near as fast as the last one, but he missed it. He felt slow and sluggish.

On his next turn at bat, when he hit a ball through the hole at third, he barely managed to reach first ahead of the throw. It wasn't one of his better days.

After the game, the walk home seemed to take forever. Gilbert paused across the street from his house. He lived on a busy road. Cars rushed by in both directions. There were breaks when he could cross, but Gilbert was afraid to try. He didn't think he could make it. He waited.

Finally, right after a red sports car whooshed past him, he saw there was nothing coming in either direction. Gilbert took a step.

At least, that's what he tried to do. His brain told his leg to step. But Gilbert couldn't move.

"I'm gummed up." That's what his brain told his mouth to say. But even his mouth wasn't moving. He could breathe, and he could think, but everything else was gummed up and stuck.

"Gilbert, hey, wait for me."

The call came from his left. He couldn't turn his head, or even move his eyes, but he recognized the voice. It was Damon. Gilbert could wait for him. That part was easy, since he really had no other choice.

"What's up?" Damon asked. The voice was close now. Right next to him.

"I'm stuck." Again, the words didn't leave Gilbert's brain.

Damon walked into view. "Are you angry or something?" He leaned closer. "It wasn't my fault we crashed into each other."

Gilbert couldn't even blink. Damon's face was so close, Gilbert could see the purple wad of gum he was chewing, and smell the faded grape aroma.

"Okay, be like that," Damon said. He plucked the gum from his mouth and stuck it on Gilbert's nose.

Gilbert's angry shout remained in his head. Damon walked off. In another moment, he'd turned the corner and moved out of sight.

"Hey, look, a gum post. How convenient."

Right after Gilbert heard the voice, he saw a man walk over to him from across the street. The man reached in his own mouth, plucked out his gum, and stuck it on Gilbert's forehead.

"I'm not a gum post!" Gilbert tried to say.

But the next three people who came along seemed to think otherwise. They also stuck their gum on Gilbert.

This can't last forever, he thought. Sooner or later the gum he'd swallowed had to get unstuck or digested or something.

A little boy came into sight, walking next to his mother.

"Look, Mommee! A gum post!" He plucked his gum out of his mouth and reached toward Gilbert's leg.

"No, dear," his mother said. "That's very unsightly. And unsanitary. Think of all the germs that could infest it." She snatched the gum from his hand.

"Thank you," Gilbert tried to say. Finally, someone with common sense had come along. A tingle of hope twitched through his gummed-up stomach, though even the tingle moved at a slow pace. Maybe the woman would help him.

"You must dispose of the gum properly," the woman said. She grabbed Gilbert's jaw and pulled down. Then she flicked the gum into his open mouth. "See. That's how these things are supposed to be used."

"Yay!" the boy said. "This is fun. I'm bringing my gum here every day. And I'm telling all my friends."

They walked off. Gilbert stayed where he was, stuck in place.

THE SNOW GLOBE

found the snow globe in a box in the attic. I guess it had been my grandfather's, because the rest of the stuff in the box was his. The glass globe was about the size of a softball, but a lot heavier. There was a snowman inside. He looked kind of creepy. I liked that.

I gave the globe a shake, but nothing happened. I guess it was so old that the fake snowflakes had gotten stuck or something.

I took it downstairs to show my younger brother, Shawn.

"Let me try." He grabbed the globe and gave it a hard shake.

A couple flakes swirled through the liquid. But not many.

"It doesn't work," Shawn said. He tossed the globe back to me.

I shook it again, and got several more flakes. I was about to put the globe away, when I looked out the window. There were some snowflakes falling through the air.

It was July.

I went outside to make sure the flakes weren't actually

flower blossoms or bits of ash. I put my hand out. One of the flakes landed on my palm. It glistened for an instant, and then melted. I felt the tiniest chill on the spot where it had landed.

Snow. For sure. I felt a bigger chill run through my body.

"Shawn!" I yelled.

He came running out. "What?"

"Watch this." I shook the globe harder than before. A little more snow swirled through the liquid. And more snow fell from the clouds.

"Wow," Shawn said. "Let me try."

I passed the globe to him. He gave it a shake. He got a few more flakes, but I could tell most of the snow was still stuck to the bottom. I took the globe back and gave it a whack on the side, making sure not to hit it so hard that it broke.

Some of the clumped snow broke free. I whacked the globe again, then shook it as hard as I could.

The globe filled with snow.

So did the sky.

Snow fell thick and heavy. A moment later, I heard the screech of brakes, and then a crash. I heard other crashes as the falling snow turned everything into a slippery slushy mess. People weren't expecting snow. Nobody had salted the road or put down cinders.

"Stop!" I shouted at the globe. That was stupid. It couldn't hear me. The snow in the globe swirled in every direction. The air around me swirled with snow. It looked like it was going to snow for a long time.

I heard another crash. People were shouting and crying.

I had to stop the snow. I lifted the globe high above my head, then hurled it down, smashing it on the ground. The globe shattered into a thousand pieces. The contents spilled out, splashing across the driveway, carrying the snowman along like he'd been tossed in a river.

The snow stopped falling.

"I did it, Shawn," I said. "Look—it stopped."

Shawn's reply was drowned out by a roar, like a thousand jet engines or a million freight trains. The sky turned dark as a wall of water raced toward us, higher than the tallest houses. The flood I'd created crashed down like a liquid hammer, knocking me off my feet and sweeping me along the road.

I tried to swim to the surface, but it seemed impossibly beyond my reach. I knew I'd never make it. As I remembered the tiny snowman being washed across my driveway, I wondered how far the flood would spread, and how far away it would carry me.

THE IRON WIZARD
GOES A-COURTIN'

There is an old saying about having too many irons in the fire. It used to make sense, back when pieces of iron were commonly heated in fires by blacksmiths. That was a long time ago.

There's an even older saying: Be careful what you wish for. That one makes as much sense now as it did back then, because people often make wishes without thinking about the consequences.

Far back, even earlier than when either of those sayings was first uttered, there lived a princess of extraordinary beauty and uncommon brilliance. Her name was Lendina, and she had a secret. She also had dozens of suitors who wished for her hand, both because of her beauty, and because anyone who marries a princess becomes a prince. At a time when most people had little to eat except for moss and frogs, princes enjoyed a very nice lifestyle.

On the first day of spring, the traditional day in the Kingdom of Wellandia for seeking hands in marriage, fifteen knights, five dukes, two peasants, and one wizard set out for the castle of King Harlis.

Only the wizard arrived at his destination. All of the other suitors met with various sorts of accidents. Strangely enough, all of the accidents seemed to involve unpleasant encounters with some form of iron. The knights who were dressed in armor or chain mail had been squeezed or constricted in ways that are best left undescribed unless one has a fascination with the grinding of meat. The fates of the other travelers were no less unpleasant—especially those who stumbled into pits filled with iron spikes, or those who were struck by iron orbs that rained from the sky like merciless hailstones.

"I come to ask for your daughter's hand in marriage," the wizard said when he was led into the great hall of the castle to meet King Harlis.

"Others have perished facing the trials she places before them," the king said. "For five springs now, suitors have come, and for four springs, they have failed to win her hand."

There was a hint of a smile on the king's lips. Although he was, for the most part, a kind and gentle ruler, he enjoyed a bit of clever perishing on occasion—especially if the perishing happened during a beautiful spring day. His own rise to power hadn't been achieved without a dash of excitement, a scattering of lost limbs, and a handful of severed heads.

"Others don't have control over the elements of the earth," the wizard said. "Behold." He pointed to the floor. A large stone at his feet shimmered, then turned to iron. Next, he pointed to a lance mounted on the wall. With a shriek of metal against metal, the lance tied itself into a knot.

"Impressive," the king said. "You have my permission to seek my daughter's hand." Still smiling, he rose from his seat and left the great hall. His smile grew larger, and became a laugh before he reached his chambers.

A moment later, Princess Lendina entered and took a seat. "You wish my hand in marriage?"

The wizard bowed low. "I do. Your beauty surpasses even the most amazing tales that have spread across the kingdom. And you could not choose a better suitor to be your prince. I am the most powerful wizard in the land." He made mystical, magical gestures in the direction of another weapon on the wall.

"There's no need for demonstrations," the princess said. "I can tell that you are powerful. But are you powerful enough? My prince must be able to protect me against all dangers."

"I am truly powerful enough," he said.

"We'll see. I will have you face one test that will challenge both your powers and your courage. If you pass, you may have my hand in marriage." She rose from her seat. "It will take time to prepare the test. Come to the northern court-yard tomorrow at sunrise."

"I'll be there," the wizard said.

The princess went to talk with the royal blacksmith, who knew all about bellows and fire, and with the royal tutor, who was well versed in all matters related to the elements of the earth. The blacksmith and the tutor went right to work, con-structing the test. They also smiled frequently.

At sunrise the next day, the princess waited at the court-yard. Extending in front of her was a walkway, forty paces long, lined with a brick wall on either side. The far end of the walkway contained a fire of small branches and twigs. With each pace, the branches grew larger and the fire grew hotter. After ten paces, the fire was fueled by logs. Ten paces beyond that, the fire was fed with coal. The last ten paces were also fed with coals. But in that stretch, men stood ready at a series of bellows that would pump air through holes in the wall, stoking the flames to even greater heat.

The wizard approached. "I am ready for the challenge," he said.

"Walk along the path I have laid out," Princess Lendina said. "Reach me, and you shall win my hand."

"And so I shall," the wizard said.

"Oh, there's a rule you must obey," the princess said. "Until we are wed, you must vow never to use magic when we are close enough to touch hands."

"This I vow," he said.

The wizard stared at the fire for a moment, as if making calculations. Then he raised his hands, whispered ancient words, and cast his most powerful spell.

His whole body turned to iron. But it was iron that was jointed where human bone was jointed. The iron bones were layered with iron muscles and iron tendons. All of this was covered with iron flesh.

The iron wizard took a step, and then another. He walked across the fire of twigs and branches as if he were strolling through a meadow of buttercups. He passed through the log fire with equal ease. As he moved through the coal fire, his iron skin flushed with tinges of red. When he reached the hottest, coal-fed, bellows-stoked stretch, he glowed a cherry red. So intense was the heat that the air around him rippled.

He moved more slowly with each step, as if the spell took greater concentration as the temperature rose. He walked the last ten paces at barely a crawl. Finally, he moved beyond the fire, reaching the waiting princess.

"Well done," she said. "But remember your vow." She extended her hand toward him, as if to remind him not to use magic when they were close enough to touch.

The wizard raised his arms, casting off the spell that had turned him to iron.

Alas, he released the spell when his iron skin was still glowing. Red-hot iron will eventually cool. Red-hot skin does not fare so well. The wizard had barely enough time for a short scream before his flesh was turned to cinders.

The princess wrinkled her nose and stepped back. Each year, the first day of spring seemed to bring a more powerful, and more stupid, wizard seeking her hand. They killed off worthy suitors, and they made a mess of the castle, bending perfectly good lances with their ridiculous spells, and showing off in all sorts of destructive ways.

Princess Lendina hated wizards. That was her secret. But she'd never tell. The iron wizard might have guessed this secret at the very last instant of his life. But he'd never tell, either.

FORTUNATE ACCIDENTS

Somewhere between the time he went flying over his handlebars and the time he landed helmet-first on the pavement twenty yards away, Keaton realized he'd messed up. *Shoulda looked . . .*

That was his last thought before he woke up in the hospital. Now he thought, *Where am I?*

He had a needle in his arm, attached to a thin plastic tube. His eyes followed the tube up to a bag of clear liquid hanging from a metal stand. There were wires attached to his chest with sticky pads. It felt like there might be more wires on his head. Behind him, he heard a beep that seemed to match the rhythm of his thumping heart.

A motion caught his attention. A man stood by the door, but he wasn't dressed like a doctor. He was wearing a suit.

"How are you feeling?"

"Okay, I guess. Was I in an accident?"

"You rode your bicycle right in front of my car. There was no way I could avoid hitting you."

Keaton wasn't sure whether he should apologize, so he

didn't say anything. People could get pretty upset if their cars were scratched or dented. He knew that from experience.

"You're very lucky," the man said. He swept his hand around. "I have my own medical facility. Let's say it was a fortunate accident that I was the one who hit you, and that you were less than a mile from my estate. I doubt you would have survived a trip all the way to the nearest trauma center."

His own hospital? Keaton realized the guy must be rich. Accident victims sometimes got lots of money. He knew that from watching television. Maybe he could get some money for himself—assuming he lived long enough. "Am I going to be okay?" he asked.

"Except for a few scratches and bruises, you're just fine now. We had to work fast to reduce the swelling that was endangering your brain, but everything went smoothly. I have the finest medical team in the state. It's also a good thing you were wearing a helmet." The man picked up a folder. "I just got the last of the results. Again, it's all quite fortunate. Despite the impact, none of your vital organs was damaged."

Keaton wanted to find out how rich the guy was. "Why do you have your own hospital?"

"I've been sick for a while," the man said. "Since birth, actually. You can't tell it from looking at me, but I don't have a lot of time left."

Keaton figured he should say something sympathetic, but he wasn't good at that sort of stuff.

"Bad heart," the man said. "An unfortunate accident of birth. You could say I was born to both fortune and misfortune. I have enormous riches, but a very poor heart."

Maybe he'll leave me some money, Keaton thought. He

moaned to let the man know how much he was hurting. Then he said, "Did you call my parents?"

The man ignored the question. "I expect I'll be dead in a month or two."

A wild thought hit Keaton. He could hear the heart monitor racing as he spat out the words. "You aren't taking my heart for yourself, are you?"

The man laughed. "Of course not. I'd have to be terribly evil to do something like that. I assure you—I'm not that evil. I've lived a full life. I'm ready for my fate."

"That's a relief." Keaton tried to calm down. He realized he'd watched too many late-night movies with evil doctors and heartless villains. "Was my bike wrecked?"

"Totally crushed," the man said.

"I guess I'll need a new one." Keaton waited for the man to take the hint.

"It's difficult going through life with a bad heart," the man said. "I was never allowed to ride a bicycle. I never got to run and play. No sports. No amusement parks."

Keaton tried again. "That bike was really expensive. I guess I'll have to walk everywhere now. At least, until I can save up enough money for a new one."

"Don't worry about it," the man said.

Finally. "So you'll buy me another bike?" Keaton asked.

The man pulled something small from his pocket. "You won't be needing a bicycle."

"Why?" The beeps sped up again.

The man smiled at Keaton, but there was nothing friendly in his expression.

I have to get out of here, Keaton thought. He looked around the room, in search of the best escape route. The man was standing between him and the door. There were several windows to his right, but Keaton had no idea what floor he was on. He looked over to his left. That's when he noticed the second bed.

"Who is that for?" he asked.

"Oh, that's mine." The man crossed the room.

"Then who is *this* for?" Keaton pointed at the bed he was on. As he braced himself to dive off the side, he wondered how much it would hurt when he ripped free from the tube and wires.

"That's the one my son uses. Unfortunately, he inherited my condition. He's much sicker than I am." The man reached up to the bag by Keaton's bedside. "But thanks to a fortunate accident, I found a young and healthy donor who has a strong heart and the right rare blood type."

"Donor?" Keaton asked.

"Yes, a donor. The odds against it were millions to one. Sometimes you get lucky. Well, actually, I guess I got lucky. And my son got lucky. But you seem to have had an unfortunate accident." The man injected something into the bag.

Keaton tried to sit up, but he was far too sleepy to move. The beeps got slower. Much slower.

"Accidents happen," the man said. "Thank goodness for that."

Those were the last words Keaton heard.

BIG BANG

I found Chelsea in her backyard. Actually, she was in the toolshed at the very back of her yard. Her parents didn't keep much stuff there, so Chelsea had dragged an old chair and table from her basement, and set them up inside. She called it her "think tank." Chelsea is so smart, it's scary.

When I walked up to the door of the shed, she didn't even seem to notice me. She was staring at some stuff on the table. I waited. She sighed, but still kept her gaze on the table.

There wasn't much to see—an old watch, a rubber band, a couple batteries, a scattering of paper clips, some tiny springs that looked like they came from ballpoint pens, and some other junk I didn't recognize. It reminded me of the random stuff I found each year when I cleaned out my desk on the last day of school.

I cleared my throat.

Chelsea frowned, but still didn't look up.

I coughed.

She lifted her head. "Oh . . . hi, Amanda."

"Hi." I stepped into the shed. The floor was a couple inches above the ground. "What are you doing?"

"I think I figured it out," she said.

"Figured what out?" I asked.

"*It*," she said, as if that tiny word could contain a huge meaning. "Everything. The secret of the universe."

I wasn't sure I'd even understand whatever she was going to tell me, but I had a feeling it was important. For the last three months, she'd been talking about bosons, leptons, neutrinos, and other things I'd never heard of before. Last week, she'd said something about being able to scrape radium—whatever that was—from the hands of very old watches. I waited for her to continue.

"If I'm right, everything can be explained in an incredibly simple way. And that's how it should be. The deep truths are simple. So simple that they're easy to overlook. That's where physics has stumbled for so long. The researchers are adding layers of complexity when they should have been seeking simplicity. Do you see?"

She was already starting to lose me, but I nodded. "So, if you've figured everything out, that's great, right?"

She pointed to the objects on the table. "I need to run an experiment to prove my theory," she said. "But if I'm right, the chain reaction initiated by my experiment will destroy the universe."

I stopped breathing as I tried to think of some way to convince myself I had misheard her. My mind churned until my lungs ached. Finally, I took a breath. My lungs felt better, but my gut felt worse. "Destroy the universe?"

"Yeah. It's an unfortunate side effect." She pointed to a

button with a couple wires attached to it. The other end of the wires was taped to a battery. Between the button and the battery, the wires snaked through an assortment of electronic parts.

"You call the end of the universe a side effect?" I backed away a step, almost stumbling at the drop-off by the entry-way. "Take it apart. Forget about it."

"But it's the answer to everything," she said. "Do you know how long physicists have been trying to unify the fields? Do you have any idea what a mess the obsession with string theory has made out of theoretical physics? This will clear up everything. I'll have a couple seconds, maybe even five or ten, to know I'm right before the end comes."

"Chelsea, you're sounding crazy. You can't do this. Come on. Get out of that shed. Come stand in the sunlight. Feel how wonderful the world is." I held out my hand and backed away a step, as if trying to coax a puppy out of a box.

Chelsea stared down at the table, and then back at me.

"Sunshine, flowers, kittens," I said. "Ice cream, new clothes, bubble bath. Think of all the great things you'd miss."

Chelsea swallowed, nodded, then stood up and walked out of the shed.

"You can't destroy the universe," I said. I couldn't believe I actually had to explain something that was so obvious.

"I guess not."

"Maybe there's another way to test your theory," I said. I figured I could distract her, and cheer her up a bit as I led her away from the shed. "Or maybe someone else will figure all of this out."

"Someone else!" Chelsea dived back into the shed. "No! Then I'd never know the truth. Not if they ended the universe. I can't let someone beat me to the answer. I have to know if I'm right."

"Don't do it!" I screamed.

Chelsea pushed the button.

I flinched, expecting some sort of terrible explosion. For an instant, nothing happened. Then I saw a tiny spot of total darkness hovering above the table. It was barely larger than a pinhead. It started to expand.

"Yes!" Chelsea screamed. "I was right. See, it's exactly what I predicted."

The sphere of blackness was the size of a golf ball now. I grabbed Chelsea's arm and tugged at it.

"You can't outrun it," she said. "It will expand exponentially until there's nothing left on the outside. That doesn't matter. I understand everything. I know the secret of the universe."

I turned and ran. Behind me, Chelsea kept talking, spewing a stream of words about subatomic particles. Then, suddenly, the sound of her voice was cut off. I didn't look back. I kept running. I knew it was pointless, but I couldn't help myself. Maybe that was the real secret of the universe. Even as the universe itself was being swallowed by blackness, life tried to find a way out. Life fought. Life never gave up.

A wall of darkness shot past me. I expected everything to go black, but the inside of the sphere wasn't dark. It was shimmery, like a soap bubble. I looked back. Chelsea was there. Everything was there. I looked ahead. The sphere was expanding, revealing more and more as it swelled away from us. In a moment, I could see all the way down the street.

Chelsea came out of the shed and stood next to me as I watched the inside of the sphere fly past the clouds.

"I was wrong," she said. "We're still here."

"That's sort of a good thing," I said.

I expected her to agree. Instead, she turned back toward the shed. "Wait. I know my mistake. I can get this to work."

I grabbed her arm. "Can you hold off for a little? You don't want to make another mistake."

"But I really need to see if I'm right."

"They're having sidewalk sales at the mall," I said. "We can try on skirts."

"Skirts?" Her gaze wavered between the shed and me.

"Yeah. Skirts. Lots of skirts. And the Freezie Shack has a new flavor this week—peach ripple. Jillian got a kitten yesterday. We could go see her on the way to the mall."

"I guess the experiment can wait," Chelsea said. "I love kittens."

I grabbed her arm and dragged her away from the shed before she changed her mind. Once I got her into the world, with its warm sunshine and blue sky, its ice cream and kittens, I was pretty sure I could convince her to hold off from doing any more experiments. Sure, it might be nice to know the secret of the universe, but nowhere near as nice as peach ripple ice cream in a waffle cone.

It looked like I'd saved the universe. I just hoped there wasn't anyone else out there like Chelsea, who was willing to destroy the universe in order to briefly understand it. Or if there was, I hoped she had a friend like me.

LAPS

Two wrongs make a right," Joey said as he read the long
list of regulations printed in large red letters on a sign
next to the pool-room door. The third and fourth rules were
the two wrongs he was about to violate.

No swimming alone.

Nobody under 16 allowed in the pool without an adult.

He'd noticed the sign on the way in, as he'd followed his
parents past the pool to the elevator. Fortunately, they hadn't
bothered to look. He knew that because when he asked if he
could go for a swim, they'd both said it was okay. All they
wanted to do was relax in the hotel room after their long
drive.

Joey didn't care about the regulations. He was a good swimmer. A serious swimmer. He wasn't going to do anything stupid, like dive headfirst into the shallow end. He checked the
hallway in both directions to make sure no hotel people
were nearby, then slipped through the entrance to the in-
door pool.

"Warm." Joey wiped sweat from his forehead. The air around the pool was hot and humid. The sharp scent of chlorine burned his nostrils. He tested the water with his toe. It was warm, too.

He climbed down the ladder at the side of the pool and waded through the chest-deep water to the shallow end. Then he pulled down his goggles and kicked off, starting with a breaststroke. After ten easy laps, he switched to free-style and picked up his pace.

As he turned his head to the side for a breath on the fifth lap, he noticed that the room had gotten steamier. In the middle of the sixth lap, he slowed to a drift and raised his head.

The air was so dense, he could barely see the side of the pool.

Bad ventilation, he thought as he resumed swimming. He didn't like breathing the damp air. But he had only four more laps of freestyle, followed by ten of the butterfly and ten of the backstroke, and then he could get out.

As he kicked off the wall on his next-to-last lap, he realized he couldn't even see the sides of the pool through the steam. He stroked cautiously, afraid to ram his head into the far wall or hit the concrete with his hand. Normally, he had a good sense of exactly where he was in a pool, and where the wall was, but something felt different here.

Maybe that's enough for one night, he thought.

Joey rolled on his side and did slow strokes with his left arm, keeping his right hand out in front. With each stroke, he expected to feel the smooth tiles of the wall. His hand met nothing. He made a quarter turn and tried to swim the short way across the pool. After more than enough strokes to cross the pool a half dozen times, Joey stopped swimming and treaded water.

He pushed up his goggles. The air was still dense. "Hey!" he shouted. He no longer cared about getting in trouble. He wanted someone to show up and yell at him to get out of the pool.

Nobody answered.

"Hey! Anybody!" His shout wavered in his throat.

Again, no answer. Worse, something sounded wrong about his voice. He let out a loud shout. "Hey!"

The cry didn't echo back at him off the walls or ceiling.

Joey raised his hands above his head, exhaled all the air in his lungs, and sank, trying to see how deep the pool was. He was pretty sure that even the oldest hotel pools built more than a century ago rarely went deeper than eight feet—twelve at most. He could easily go that far.

He went much farther, but failed to find the bottom. Joey stroked back to the surface. When he broke into the opaque air, he realized the water was rolling all around him, rising and falling in gentle swells as if pushed by a distant wind. It didn't seem like he was in a pool. It almost seemed like—no, Joey shook his head at the impossibility of that. But the thought wouldn't go away.

There was one sure way to tell. He didn't want to know. But he had to find out.

He touched a wet finger to his tongue.

Salt.

He sniffed carefully, then inhaled deeply, but he already knew what he'd find. There was no strong scent of chlorine in the air. No pool smell. If anything, the air smelled of salt and seaweed.

Joey put his goggles back over his eyes and rolled forward, starting another slow crawl. He knew it was pointless, but he couldn't think of anything else to do.

Joey swam. Around him, the water lapped at his arms and legs, patient, waiting.

BEDBUGS

Don't let the bedbugs bite," Dad said as the bus pulled into the rec center parking lot.

I laughed, even though it wasn't really funny. Behind Dad, Grandma gave me a wink and a nod. I winked back and patted my pocket to let her know I had the bottle.

"Have fun," Mom said. "Be careful."

"I will." I figured that answered both her sentences. Around me, a herd of kids charged toward the bus as the doors opened.

"This is going to be great," Bobby Epstein said as he grabbed my shoulder and pulled me into the mob.

"For sure." I pushed my way onto the bus, along with the rest of the kids. Our youth group was going to New York City for an overnight trip. Today, we'd get to go to the science museum, and then have dinner at a real New York restaurant. Tomorrow, we'd see a Broadway show in the afternoon before heading back home.

It was about a two-hour ride from South Jersey up to New York. Most of us had been to the city before, but Bobby was just about the only one who had ever stayed there. Him and Trent Parnell.

"We stayed at the Ritz," Trent said. "It's the most expensive hotel in all of New York. We had a suite. That's a whole bunch of rooms, all just for us. I had my own bed. It was king size. There was a TV in every single room. Even the bathroom!"

I didn't bother listening. Trent always bragged about having the most expensive or the biggest or the best of everything.

"My dad and I stayed at the YMCA. It was fun." Bobby held up the sheet of paper that listed our schedule. "I don't know this hotel."

"It's whatever Mr. Drampner picked out," I said.

Mr. Drampner was in charge of the youth group. He ran the sports and picked the movies for movie night. He did a pretty good job, but sometime he'd try to get the cheapest stuff to save money. I glanced at the sheet in Bobby's hand. I'd never heard of the hotel, either. But that didn't mean anything. There were a zillion hotels in New York.

After we came out of the tunnel, we headed downtown. It took a long time to get through the city traffic to our hotel.

"Ick," Trent said as we got off the bus. "This place is a dump."

I had to agree—it didn't look very nice from the outside. The windows were dirty, and the walls were covered with graffiti. It was a little better inside.

"At least it seems kind of clean," Bobby said.

"I guess it's not bad." The rugs were worn out and the wallpaper was peeling, but someone had vacuumed recently, and there wasn't any sort of bad smell.

Mr. Drampner got the room keys and handed them out.

We were staying two kids in a room, except for Trent, who made a big fuss about not wanting to have to share a room since he had his own room at home. Luckily, there was an odd number of kids, so he got to be by himself. Bobby and I stuck together, of course.

"Cool!" Bobby said when we went into our room. "It's got a big TV."

He bounced on one of the beds.

"Careful," I said. "Check it for bedbugs."

"Are you serious?" he asked.

"For sure." After Grandma had warned me about bedbugs, I'd actually looked them up online. It was a big problem in some hotels. And not just in cities. They were showing up all over the place. "The thing is, you don't even feel it when they bite you. But you'll itch like crazy later."

I pulled back the bedspread and checked the sheets. "They say you should look for little blood spots."

"That's gross," Bobby said.

"Maybe, but it's not as gross as getting bitten all night and having them drink your blood."

"I guess." Bobby pulled down the cover on his bed. "So what do you do if you see spots?"

"You can ask for another room," I said.

"Except the whole place is full," he said. "They closed off all the rooms on the top two floors because of a bad leak in the roof, and our group took all the rest of the rooms."

"Right." The clerk had told us that when we checked in. I bent over and took a close look at the sheets. They were pretty worn. It was hard to tell if there were any tiny spots. I pulled the bottle from my pocket. "Just to be safe, my grandma gave me this."

"What is it?"

"Neem oil," I said.

"Never heard of it."

"Me, neither. Not until yesterday. But she swears it keeps bedbugs away. Can't hurt, right?"

I pulled the cork from the top of the bottle. A strong smell nearly knocked me over.

"Oh, man," Bobby said. "That will keep everything away—bedbugs, elephants, asteroids. Phewww!" He pinched his nose.

I stuck the cork back, which cut down on the smell, though some of it lingered in the air. I put the bottle down on the dresser, then glanced at the clock. "Come on. It's time to meet up."

We joined the others and rode the subway to the museum, which was awesome, and the restaurant, which wasn't all that good. Then we went back to the hotel. When we got to the lobby, I told everyone, "Wait here for a minute. Okay?"

I dashed to my room, got the bottle of neem oil, and returned to the lobby. "This keeps away bedbugs," I said. "Anyone want some?"

I opened the bottle, put some of the oil on my hands, and rubbed it on my neck and arms. I have to admit, I got a kick out of how bad it smelled. It was sort of like a challenge.

One or two kids stepped right up. And then the rest of them joined in. Even Mr. Drampner took some. The only one who didn't was Trent.

"You guys are idiots," he said. "Stinky idiots."

I ignored him. And I slept well that night. So did Bobby. We woke up when my phone alarm went off. We were supposed to all meet for breakfast.

As I rolled out of bed, the strong smell of neem oil reminded me I'd been worried about bedbugs. I didn't feel itchy. That was good. I checked my arms and chest. No bites.

"Any itches?" I asked Bobby.

He paused for a moment, then shook his head. "Nope. That stuff worked great. Tell your grandma I said thanks."

"Sure." We headed down to the lobby. In a couple minutes, everyone was there except for Trent. Mr. Drampner called his room. There was no answer.

He got the manager and they went down the hall toward Trent's room. The rest of us followed. With each step, I grew more worried.

"The neem oil kept the bedbugs away from us," I said to Bobby.

"Yup. It definitely did."

"And everyone except for Trent used it, right?"

Bobby nodded. Then he froze. I guess he'd figured it out, too. "Uh-oh. They had to go somewhere. . . ."

"Yeah, that's what I'm thinking."

By then, we'd reached the door of Trent's room. The manager knocked real hard, waited a moment, then unlocked the door and opened it. Mr. Drampner stepped inside. I pushed in behind him.

There was something on the bed. It looked like a balloon that had lost about half its air. I gasped as I realized it was Trent. Or what was left of him after all the bedbugs in the entire hotel had been forced into one room.

"I guess we're not going to see the play," Bobby said.

"Trent's definitely not going," I said.

"It probably isn't a good play, anyhow," Bobby said.

I glanced at the faded carpet and peeling wallpaper in the hallway, and thought about the dinner we'd had last night. "You're right. It's probably not very good." If we missed it, that was fine with me. I was ready to go back home and wash up. I still smelled like neem, but at least I had all my blood, and no itchy spots.

THE VALLEY
OF LOST TREASURES

Mom, have you seen my roller skates?" Mandy called. She was on her hands and knees, halfway inside her bedroom closet, searching through a jumbled mess of over-stuffed boxes and scattered clothing. The jungle of pants and dresses hanging from the rod above made the search even tougher.

"Did you look in your closet?" her mom called from the kitchen.

"Great suggestion," Mandy muttered. She sighed, backed out of the closet, and sat on the floor. *Where can they be?* She looked under her bed. The skates weren't there. Lots of magazines, plenty of shoes, enough dust bunnies to stuff a pillow, but no skates.

After another half hour of searching, Mandy gave up and called her friend Charlotte. "I can't go skating."

"Why not?"

"I can't find my skates," she said.

"You can rent skates," Charlotte said. "It's not expensive."

"I don't feel like skating today. I'll go with you next time."

Mandy didn't think it would be as much fun without her skates. They fit perfectly. And they were made of real leather. But maybe they wouldn't even fit now. She hadn't worn them in months.

As Mandy headed downstairs, she thought about some of her other favorite things. She hadn't been able to find her stuffed lamb last month when she was doing a multimedia biography for a school project. *I haven't seen Lammie in years,* she thought. It wasn't just the lamb and the skates. A week ago, she'd looked all over the house for a special pen her aunt had given her.

As she reached the bottom of the stairs, she saw something glitter. Behind the steps, right by the door to the basement, she spotted one of her favorite hair clips. As she bent to reach for it, she realized there was no way it could have gotten there. It had been in a drawer in the bathroom cabinet. She'd put it there on Saturday evening, and she knew she hadn't worn it since then.

Something weird was happening. Mandy decided to leave the clip where it was. The next day, it was gone. She opened the basement door and switched on the light. She checked all the steps as she walked down, and then hunted around until she found the clip along the side wall, several feet past the stairs.

It moved, she thought. It almost seemed as if the clip was going somewhere. Mandy wondered where a clip could possibly want to go. There was no way she could stay in the basement and watch it all night. Even if she waited, she had a feeling the clip would never move while she was looking at it.

Maybe she could track it. She went upstairs and scooped a

quarter cup of flour out of the canister her mom kept on the kitchen counter. She ran back down, half afraid the clip would have moved again, or maybe disappeared.

But it was there. She sprinkled a dusting of flour on the floor around it. Now, if it moved, there'd be a trail.

The next morning, Mandy checked the basement as soon as she woke up. She gasped when she realized the clip was gone. She could see signs that it had moved through the flour. She followed the streaky trail to the corner of the basement, beneath an old table.

She crawled under the table and touched the wall. Instead of the cold hard feel of concrete, her fingers met something like velvet. She pushed her arm through. There was emptiness on the other side.

Mandy crawled through the softness of the wall.

It was brighter on the other side. She was in a large field of grass. Ahead, she saw all sorts of objects scattered across the ground.

My things!

She spotted her skates right away. One was up on all four wheels; the other lay on its side, as if the journey had exhausted it. Nearby, she saw her pen.

She strolled among the lost treasures—things she knew were missing and things she didn't even realize she'd lost. The farther she walked, the older the things became. At the far end of the field, where it met a stream, she found things she didn't even remember owning. There were baby toys, clothes, a board book with teeth marks on the cover, and a small teddy bear.

Mandy looked ahead, and then back the way she'd come. The land seemed to stretch forever in all directions.

"Everything in here is lost," she whispered. "Everything . . ."

She looked for a path back to her house. There was nothing to see but open land.

Elsewhere, in the world she'd left, there would soon be a poster asking if anyone had seen Mandy. LOST GIRL the message at the top would read. PLEASE CALL IF YOU SEE HER.

Nobody ever saw her. Nobody ever called.

CATFISHING IN AMERICA

Every summer, I visited my cousin Vince in Alabama. I loved it. All we did was swim, fish, and go rafting. The river was Vince's playground all year round.

Vince and his folks lived right near the water. We'd taken their rowboat out to a small island that morning, and had been fishing for sunnies all day.

There are bass and some perch in the river, too. Bass are exciting to catch, but sunnies are fun because they'll bite at anything. I've even caught them on a bare hook once or twice. They go especially crazy over red worms—the skinny little ones, not the fat night crawlers—and we'd dug a ton of those in Vince's backyard, right next to his mom's vegetable garden.

As the sun started to touch the horizon, Vince reeled in his line and got up from the rock he'd been sitting on.

"Where you going?" I asked. I checked the bucket next to me. I still had tons of bait wriggling in the dirt, and there'd be plenty of light for at least another half hour.

"It's getting dark," he said. "We need to go back."

"Why?" I was having a great time.

"Catfish will come out soon," Vince said.

I couldn't help laughing. "Catfish? What are they going to do—jump out of the water and bite us?"

"Maybe," Vince said.

His voice was so flat, and his face so serious, that I felt a strange tug in my gut. I'd caught enough catfish to know you had to be careful handling them. They had these whiskers—called *barbels*—that could punch a hole into your hand. It stung real bad. They had spikes in their fins, too. And they had teeth that looked kind of like fangs. But none of that had anything to do with sunset, and none of it should have scared my cousin. "What's going on?" I asked.

"The catfish around the island—they're different. Everyone who lives here knows it, even if nobody talks about it. Come on. Let's go. We can come back tomorrow."

"No way." I slid off the fallen oak I'd been sitting on and walked over to Vince. "That's silly. Fish are fish. Whatever you heard—it's nothing more than some sort of story people tell to scare kids, like the bogeyman and all that nonsense."

"You're just a city boy. You don't understand this stuff."

"And you're just a hick," I said.

Vince gave me a push. "Them's fighting words."

I could have gotten angry, but I'd been pushed a lot harder. I go to a pretty tough school in the city, and I'd been in my share of fights. So I wasn't feeling the need to push back or to prove anything. I was more interested in seeing if I could get Vince angry.

"Thems?" I said, mocking his accent. "Where'd you learn English? A haystack? Where'd you learn biology, for that

matter? I'd call it *ichthyology*, but that's one of those big city words you wouldn't understand. I can't believe you're scared of some stupid catfish."

Vince glared at me. He was so angry, I could see his body quiver. Maybe I'd pushed him too far. I thought about what I'd just said and realized it had been way too mean. I guess it wouldn't hurt to apologize.

As I was trying to figure out the best way to tell him I was sorry, he crossed his arms and said, "All right, then, city boy. Let's stay."

He looked like someone who'd just volunteered to take part in a firing squad—and not on the shooting end.

"Nah, let's go," I said. "I'm tired of fishing." I thought back to other summers. I couldn't remember ever fishing in the river after dark. Or swimming. Vince had always found something else for us to do before the sun had fully set.

He walked over to the rowboat where we'd beached it on the bank, and gave it a push with his foot.

"Hey! Are you crazy?" I watched as it got caught by the current and swept away.

"I guess we're staying," Vince said.

I pointed downriver, where the boat had almost moved out of sight. "You lost the boat!"

Vince shook his head. "Nope. She'll wash up at the bend in the shallows just before where Nashamuk Creek feeds in. The boat's not lost. But we're stuck here until someone comes looking for us, city boy."

I watched the boat sweep around a bend. "When will that be?"

"My folks are out at the square dance," Vince said.

Before I could make a comment, he pointed a finger at me. "One joke, just one little joke about square dancing, and you'll be drifting in that current, too."

I held up my hands. "Hey, I'm not saying a word."

I picked up my rod and reached for a worm. I figured I might as well get back to fishing.

"Let's build a fire first," Vince said.

"Why?" I glanced toward the horizon, where a three-quarter moon was rising in the cloudless sky. "There's plenty of light."

Vince muttered something that didn't sound very polite and stepped into the small cluster of trees behind us. He came back five minutes later with an armful of deadwood, which he tossed to the ground with a bit more force than was necessary. "Got any matches?" he asked as he patted his pockets.

"Nope. Why would I carry matches?"

"It's always smart to carry matches," he said. "Just in case you need to make a campfire."

"I'll try to remember that the next time some idiot strands me on an island."

The sun was gone now, though the sky was still more blue than black. A dark shadow moved near the edge of the water. I stepped toward it, but Vince grabbed my shoulder. "Stay back."

I pulled away from his grip and walked over to the bank. "Whoa—it's a catfish."

That's what it was. A small one, compared to the river giants—maybe a foot long. I bent down to take a closer look.

The dark gray catfish, which was just below the surface, lifted its head out of the water, opened its mouth, and hissed at me. Yeah—it hissed. As I leaped back, I caught sight of fangs in its mouth. Four fangs—two on top and two on the bottom. They were a lot longer than any fish teeth I'd ever been this close to before.

"Did you see that?" I shouted.

"I tried to warn you," Vince said.

I could feel my heart thumping in my chest. I took a breath and told myself there was nothing to worry about. "It's just a fish."

"There'll be more," Vince said. "And they'll be bigger. The small ones aren't smart enough to wait until the light is totally gone. But all of them, big or small, like to hunt for warm blood."

I looked at the river, where dark shapes gathered beneath the surface. "We have to build that fire," I said.

Vince shrugged. "I wish we could."

A couple more catfish had moved up to the shore. Then one or two wriggled onto the bank. More fish followed them.

I checked behind me. The wooded area wasn't big—maybe twenty or thirty feet across. Past that was the other bank of the island. I walked along the shore, keeping away from the catfish. I went all the way around the island. Even though I was moving slowly, watching my step for rocks and tree roots in the moonlight, it didn't take more than five or ten minutes.

"They're coming out all around us," I said. I grabbed one of the sticks from Vince's pile. "Maybe we can beat them off."

I walked toward the closest fish and took a swing. The fish snapped at the stick, biting off the end.

"This is crazy!" I shouted. "Vampire fish? No. I'm not going to accept that. And I'm sure not going to let anything suck out all my blood on a stupid island in the middle of a stupid river."

Vampire fish.

My mind churned with ideas, trying to think of a way out. We could swim for the bank, but if the river was filled with those fish, we were just handing ourselves to them.

"Okay," I said, talking as much to myself as to Vince. "How do you kill vampires?"

"Wooden stake," Vince said. He tapped the fishing knife on his belt, then pointed to the piece of wood I'd dropped. "I could whittle a point on it."

"We'll need a whole lot more than one stake," I said. Dozens of the catfish had moved onto the shore and were wriggling toward us. I figured they'd reach us in another minute or two. "We could climb a tree," I said. "And stay there until sunrise."

Vince sighed. "I think they can climb, too. I found a dead squirrel in a tree by the river last year. It had been sucked dry."

I almost gave up. But I thought about all those vampire movies where the vampire sizzles and crackles in the light of the sun. The real sun was hours away. But these weren't real vampires. They were fish vampires. So maybe I could hurt them, or hold them off, with a different sun.

I grabbed my rod, baited the hook with a red worm, and cast over the catfish into the current.

Two seconds later, I felt a tap on my line. A small tap. Perfect.

Don't mess up.

This was something I'd done a thousand times before, without thinking. Now it was hard not thinking what would happen if I failed. I tried not to let my mind get in the way of my reflexes. Luckily, I managed to time things just right.

I set the hook and reeled in the line, giving it a yank as

the fish reached the bank. It flew over the catfish and landed in my waiting hand.

I held it up high and hoped I was right.

The moonlight glinted off the sunfish. The scales sparked like dazzling gems. The catfish hissed and gasped. They wriggled away, turning back toward the water. A couple of the smaller ones rolled on their sides, thrashed like they'd been stabbed, and burst into flames.

Vince took a branch over to a burning catfish and held it against the body until the stick caught fire. He used that to get the rest of the woodpile blazing.

I held up the sunnie until I was sure all the catfish had fled. Then I unhooked the fish and put it gently back in the water. I figured I owed it a safe return.

Once I was sure the banks were clear, I joined Vince at the fire.

"Pretty smart for a city boy," he said.

"Dang . . ." That was about as much as I could say at the moment.

"Careful," he said. "You're starting to sound like a country boy."

"There are worse things." I said.

Across the river, I heard the sound of a motorboat. His folks were coming for us. We'd made it.

POSER

'd spent the morning walking around town, trying to find a summer job. No luck. Maybe I should have started looking before school ended, or during the first month of summer vacation, but I sort of put it off. Now, partway through July, it looked like all the jobs for kids had been snatched up.

I was heading home when I saw the poster. The ad was hand-printed in colored pencil on a sheet of paper that looked like it was torn from a drawing pad.

ARTIST'S MODEL NEEDED. MALE. AGE 10 TO 12. GOOD PAY IF YOU CAN STAND STILL.

There was an address at the bottom. I was pretty sure it was just a block or two away.

I realized there was a chance this could be some sort of trick. There were lots of creepy people out there. They were always warning us about that in school, and showing us safety videos with smiling people in vans who were pretending to look for lost puppies. But I wasn't going to walk into some place without making sure I was safe. I was too smart for that. I got my phone and called my friend Tyler.

"What's up?" he asked.

"I'm checking out this job. It's probably okay, but I don't want to take any chances. I'll keep my phone on. If you hear me yell or anything, hang up on me and call 911. Okay?"

"Sure. I've got you covered."

I told him the address. I really didn't think there was any sort of danger—not when the ad was posted right out there on the street, where anyone could see it—but it's always a good idea to be careful.

The place was right where I thought it would be. The guy who answered the door looked like he was around thirty years old. He had a small paintbrush in his hand, and paint smears on the old denim shirt he was wearing. The odor of turpentine and bacon drifted out through the doorway. I guess he lived there. Past him, in a room down the hallway, I could see all sorts of artist's stuff, like an easel and a bunch of canvases.

"What do you want?" he asked.

"The job for an artist's model. That was your ad, right?"

"Oh, yeah." He stepped back and stared at me for a moment, tilting his head different ways. "You've got the perfect look. Can you stand still for an hour at a time?"

"Can I wear my earphones?" I asked.

"Sure. As long as you don't bounce around." He started to walk down the hallway, then spun back and said, "Well, don't just stand there."

I followed him in, and he put me right to work. Though it felt weird to call it work, since all I had to do was stand there with my arms raised and my fists clenched like I was banging on a wall. While he was setting up his supplies, I pulled out my phone and told Tyler everything was okay.

"So I don't get to call 911?" he asked.

"Sorry. No."

He sighed. "Maybe next time."

The artist had finished setting out his stuff, so I put my phone away. He told me his name was Caspar. No first or last name. Just Caspar.

Whatever.

He had a large sketch pad on an easel in front of him, and a piece of charcoal in his hand. "This is just a study. The real piece will come later. But it's a great commission. The most important work I've ever been asked to do."

He got quiet for a minute or two as he sketched. But then he started talking again. "The piece will be called *Child of the New Decade Raging Against the Past.*"

"Child?" I asked, trying not to move as I spoke. This reminded me of being at the dentist.

"Don't take it personally. It's just a label. The important thing is for you to look angry." He sketched some more, stepped back, stared at the pad, stepped forward, tore the page off, and let it drift to the floor. Then he started a new sketch.

And that was my workday. It was hard keeping my fists clenched for so long, but he gave me a break once in a while so I could put my arms down. He paid me in cash when we were finished.

"Is that it?" I asked.

"No. Far from it. We've just begun. There's too much at stake here to leap straight into the final stage. Every step requires thought. Tomorrow, I'll get out the paints."

That was fine with me. I was happy to know I had more money coming. My muscles were stiff from all that posing, but it wasn't any worse than some of the stuff they made us do in gym class. And I never got paid for push-ups.

During the next two days, Caspar painted a large canvas on his easel. He kept asking me to lean forward more. I tried, but it was hard keeping my balance.

The day after that, when I showed up at the studio, there was a glass box in the spot where I usually posed.

Caspar swung out one side of it, like a door. "Step in," he said.

"Why?"

"The final piece involves having you appear to be slightly off balance, and I realize you can't hold that pose. I need to get the effect just right. And I think it will help if you have something to bang your fists against. Don't worry—the glass is unbreakable."

"Okay. Sure." That made sense. Well, not really. But I'd stopped trying to understand everything he was doing, and I'd really started to enjoy the way the money piled up. Besides, it would definitely be easier posing, now that I had something to lean against. I stepped inside the box. "When is the painting due?"

Caspar closed the box. I heard something click. Then he said, "Oh, the final piece isn't a painting."

"No? What is it?"

"A sculpture," he said. He bent over and picked up a hose from the floor. He attached the hose to the bottom of the box.

"Cool." That could take weeks. The money would keep piling up. I looked around, but didn't see a big block of stone. Maybe he was going to use clay. "Are you carving it?"

"No. I'm casting it," he said. "Hold still."

I noticed a suitcase and a couple boxes stacked in the corner. As I wondered whether he was moving to another studio, I felt something wet against my legs. A thick liquid was flooding the container.

"Hey! Stop that!" I banged my fists against the glass. It didn't break.

In seconds, the liquid was up past my waist. It smelled like melted plastic. My phone had already gotten soaked. The fumes made my head spin. I banged my fists against the glass again. "Let me out!"

"Yes, perfect!" Caspar said. "Show your rage."

The liquid was up to my chin. Then it flowed over my head. I realized he was planning to use my body as a mold for his sculpture.

I tried to smash the glass, but the liquid was so thick, I couldn't build up any force. I couldn't even move my legs. Whatever this stuff was, it had already turned solid down there. A moment later, my fists were frozen in place against the glass. On the other side, through a blur of glass and plastic, I could see Caspar's fists clenched in triumph.

"Perfect!" he shouted.

I wanted to scream, but I couldn't even open my mouth to do that. Or to breathe.

I remembered something our art teacher always said in school. She even had it printed on one of her coffee cups: ART IS LONG, LIFE IS SHORT.

She had no idea how true that was.

BEWARE THE
NINJA WEENIES

Die!" Jimmy Butafesko screamed as he leaped out of a
Dumpster to my right and hurled a fistful of shuriken—
ninja throwing stars—directly at my chest. This was definitely not what I wanted to run into on the way home from a
long day of school.

"Fool! You fell into our devious trap." Isaac Swadman
dropped from a tree to my left and rushed forward, swinging
his katana.

Fortunately, the shuriken were cardboard, and the katana
was plastic. Unfortunately, Jimmy and Isaac were real. And
real annoying. Even with his face wrapped in black cloth, I
had no trouble identifying Jimmy, thanks to a unibrow that
could have been mistaken for a climbing rope. As for Isaac,
no amount of fabric could disguise his huge nose.

"Go away," I said.

"In a flash!" Jimmy threw something at the sidewalk. It
made a tiny popping sound. No flash. No smoke. But Jimmy
and Isaac squatted, pivoted away from me, and duck-walked
off as if they were hidden by vast plumes of dense smoke.

They headed down Talmadge Street, where they joined a half dozen other black-hooded kids waiting for them on the next corner.

"They were so much less annoying last month," my friend Kyle Hashimoto said as he caught up with me.

"Yeah. The pirate stuff was a pain, but this is a lot worse." Back then, all we had put up with was hearing, "Arg!" a whole bunch. *Arrrrgument. Barrrrgain. Tarrrget.* You get the idea.

But I guess the pirates were lost at sea because, for the past week or so, Jimmy, Isaac, and all their friends had become total ninja weenies, crawling, leaping, skulking, sneaking, attacking, and generally being more annoying than a swarm of horseflies on a hot day.

"At least it won't last long," Kyle said. "Those guys have the attention span of puppies."

"You're right. They'll get bored with it soon enough."

I went with Kyle to his place. His folks both work, but his grandfather was there. He doesn't speak much English. That didn't matter. I liked him, and he seemed to like me. He always gave us snacks.

"Did you ever meet a ninja?" I asked him when he brought us a plate of ginger cookies.

He laughed. "No ninjas." Then he walked off to tend his garden. He grew all sorts of plants and flowers behind the house. Once, when I had a cold, he rubbed some crushed leaves on my chest and I felt a whole lot better.

"You sure he's not a ninja?" I asked Kyle. "I've never seen anyone make so little noise when he walks."

"Right—he's a ninja. I'm a ninja. My cat is a ninja. Even the goldfish are ninjas. It's bad enough Jimmy is obsessed.

Don't you start. Let's think about important stuff, like your party."

"Good idea." My birthday was next month, and my parents were letting me throw a big party for all my friends. Kyle had already come up with a lot of great ideas.

On the way home, I passed the place where the Twirly Tykes Dance Studio used to be. It had closed more than a year ago. There was a new sign over the door announcing MASTER O'ROURKE'S NINJUTSU ACADEMY. According to a flyer in the window, they were having a grand opening on Saturday.

I snorted and walked on. I'd done some research last year for a history report on ninjas. Most of the stuff you saw about them was totally wrong. Ninjas were more like spies than superfighters. They'd disguise themselves as craftsmen or soldiers to infiltrate enemy armies. They'd start fires to distract people, and then do sabotage. They were experts in poisons and chemical weapons. But they couldn't float through the air, or perform any of the other superhuman stuff people see in movies.

Kyle and I stayed away from the grand opening. Not only did all the ninja weenies go, but as I found out on Monday in school, they'd all signed up for lessons.

"This is definitely getting out of hand," Kyle said as we walked to our class.

"For sure." I watched Jimmy try to do a wall run. He managed to go two steps before he fell. He wasn't wearing his ninja outfit, since the school had rules about that, but he'd pulled his black T-shirt up so it covered his mouth.

All around us, the ninja weenies were dashing, sneaking,

slashing, and generally turning the hallways into a pathetic version of an even more pathetic video game—the kind you can find heaped up in a bin at the bargain store for three dollars.

"What beats a ninja?" I asked after Jimmy and Isaac leaped out at me from a pair of lockers, pelted me with fake darts, and scurried away.

"Nothing I can think of," Kyle said. "Except maybe a superhero. Why?"

"I don't know. It would just be nice to see all of them whacked back into the real world, so they stop acting like ninjas."

"Won't happen," Kyle said. "Not now that they're taking lessons."

"I know, but it would be nice. Doesn't it bother you that they're stealing your culture?" I figured, being Japanese, Kyle would have a special attachment to ninjas.

"My culture? I was born in Grand Rapids, just like my dad."

"But your grandfather came here from Japan. Right?"

"Right. But even way back when he was a kid, there was no sign of ninjas. At least, not real ones."

The ninjas might have vanished ages ago, but the ninja weenies were far from gone. And they were learning some dangerous things. I guess even fake ninjas can do damage. Two weeks later, I saw Jimmy putting Dale Wertner in some kind of headlock behind the school. It looked like it hurt.

"Stop that!" I said.

"Ninjas do not take orders," Jimmy said. He let go of Dale and leaped toward me. I put my hands up to protect myself. Jimmy grabbed my arm and put me in a wristlock.

"Ouch! Let me go!"

"Pledge your allegiance to the Black Mask Clan of Master O'Rourke," he said.

"Knock it off."

He twisted harder. "Pledge!"

"Okay—you have my allegiance."

Jimmy loosened his grip. But then he bore down again. "And invite me to your party."

Oh, man. How did he know about that? I'd been real quiet about the invitations. I had plenty of friends at school, but there were some kids I just didn't want to hang out with. So I'd emailed the invitations. I guess kids at school were talking about the party because it was just a day away.

Jimmy twisted harder.

"Okay—you're invited."

He let go and dashed off.

I told Kyle the sad details on the way home from school.

"The last thing you want is Jimmy at your party."

"I know. He'll ruin it. And he'll bring all his friends." I didn't see any easy way out.

"Maybe you can talk to that ninjutsu guy," Kyle said. "He can't possibly want his students acting like this. It brings him dishonor."

"It's worth a try. Will you come with me?" I was nervous about going there by myself.

"Sure. I've been kind of curious about the place."

When we went into the ninjutsu school, there was a pale redheaded guy sitting behind a counter facing the workout area. I guess it was Master O'Rourke.

"Ah, new students. Excellent. Would you like to sign up for a single year or buy a lifetime membership?"

"Uh, actually, I wanted to talk to you about some of your

students, like Jimmy Butafesko and Isaac Swadman. They're causing a lot of trouble at school."

"Wonderful!" he said. "I've taught them well. Troublemaking is one of the seventy-five secret ninja arts I teach my students."

I glanced over at Kyle, who shrugged. I tried again. "They're going to crash my birthday party."

"I'm so proud of them," he said. "Crashing is another of the seventy-five secret ninja arts that I teach. We call it *infiltration*. So, now that you boys know two of the secrets, would you like to sign up so you can learn the other seventy-three?"

I could see this wasn't going to do any good. Before I could leave, Kyle said, "Who taught you to be a ninja?"

"I taught myself," the man said. "I have a natural gift for martial arts. I've read a lot of books and watched all the best ninja movies."

"How interesting." Kyle smiled at the man and walked out.

I hurried to catch up with him on the sidewalk. "Doesn't that guy make you angry? He's a total fake."

"Anger is a waste of energy. Forget about him. It's not worth worrying about."

I tried to forget about it, but the next day at school, all the ninja weenies kept sneaking up behind me and whispering, "See you tonight."

By lunchtime, I was ready to call home and tell my folks to forget about the party. "I give up," I told Kyle.

"Hey, don't be a quitter," he said.

I sat there and stared at my spaghetti. That's what they had on Fridays. And it was actually pretty good for cafeteria food, as long as you remembered not to eat the sausage. But I wasn't hungry.

I stared to my left, at the table full of ninja weenies. Past them, an old lady was mopping the floor. That was weird. The custodians always wait until after lunch to start mopping. I didn't recognize her, and I hadn't seen her come in. I knew all the custodians. Maybe she'd just gotten hired. As I was watching her, she dropped the mop and pointed out the window.

"Fire!" she shouted.

I raced over to the window with the rest of the kids. A pile of leaves along the curb was on fire. One of the regular custodians ran out with a fire extinguisher. He blasted the leaves with a jet of CO_2, and the fire was history.

As I walked back to my seat, I noticed the cleaning lady was moving away from Jimmy's table. There was something familiar about her walk. It was smooth and silent. I watched as she slipped into the hall.

"I'll be right back," I told Kyle.

I stepped into the hallway just in time to see the lady slip something onto her hands and climb the wall—yeah, she went straight up the wall, clinging to it like a lizard. She pushed aside a ceiling tile and vanished like chimney smoke in a sudden breeze.

"What in the world . . ."

I thought back through everything that had happened in the cafeteria. A stranger. A disguise. A fire.

"Oh, no!" I raced back to the cafeteria and ran over to Jimmy's table.

He and his friends were about to wolf down their spaghetti.

"How dare you disturb us?" Isaac said. "Ninjas do not mix with common peasants during meals."

"What do you want?" Jimmy asked. "Speak quickly or suffer."

"Nothing." I took my seat and stared at my spaghetti. Next to me, Kyle was halfway finished with his. He didn't seem worried. If my suspicion was correct, he knew a lot more than I did about what was going on. I picked up my fork and took a bite. It tasted fine. For the next two minutes, all I heard was normal cafeteria noises. Then a scream rose above the chatter.

"*Aiiieee!*"

I spun to my left, expecting to find a ninja weenie leaping at me. But Jimmy wasn't launching an attack. He was launching his lunch. And his breakfast.

He wasn't spewing alone. The rest of the ninja weenies were on their feet, too. Or their knees. Isaac was flat on the table, with his head hanging over the edge. Something had made them all sick—and only them. All around the cafeteria, I didn't see anyone else throwing up. But I saw a lot of smiles. I think Jimmy had annoyed most of the kids in school.

I put down my fork. The smell in the cafeteria had killed my appetite. I joined the rest of the kids and hustled outside, where the air was a lot fresher.

"Wow," Kyle said. "I don't think they're going to any parties tonight. I wonder what happened to them?"

"You know what happened to them," I said. "Your grandfather disguised himself as an old woman, created a distraction with a fire, and poisoned their food."

"Are you out of your mind?" Kyle jabbed a finger at my forehead. "That's ridiculous."

"He's a ninja! I know he is." I said, "They're still around. He's one. I'll bet you're training to be one, too. You're way too calm for a normal kid."

"Now you're getting even more ridiculous," Kyle said.

"Yeah, you're right," I said. "My imagination flies out of control sometimes." I started to turn away from Kyle, then spun back and threw a hard punch right at his head.

My punch didn't land. Kyle deflected it with a move so fast, it was a blur. Somehow, I was flying through the air. Kyle had flung me over his head like I was no heavier than a single-serving-size bag of potato chips.

"Sorry! You caught me by surprise. You okay?" he asked after I'd bounced to a landing on my back.

"I'm fine. But you're a . . ."

His stare cut off my words. "I'm a what?" he asked. His fingertips twitched, like he was thinking about forming fists.

"A great friend," I said. And I was happy to leave it at that. If Kyle was training to be a ninja, that was his culture, his business, and his secret. I was just happy to have him, and his grandfather, on my side. And I was happy to have the ninja weenies out of action for the moment.

On the way home from school, I saw a sign written in shaky marking pen on the door of the ninja school. *Closed due to illness.* I guess Master O'Rourke had eaten the wrong thing, too.

That night, at my party—which was totally awesome in all ways—Kyle handed me an envelope.

"What's this?" I asked.

"Your present."

I wanted to point out that he and his grandfather had already given me a present, but I'd promised not to talk about that. I opened the envelope. "Wow—thanks!" It was a gift certificate for karate lessons.

"This place teaches traditional karate. The real stuff. My grandfather picked it out," Kyle said. "A couple months of this, and you can stand up to the ninja weenies. Not that they'll still be a problem. I'm betting they'll start acting like zombies or Martians pretty soon, now that the fake school is closed. And I'm pretty sure it won't open back up."

"What about real ninjas?" I asked. "Will I be able to beat them?"

"Dream on," Kyle said. He gave me a playful punch on the shoulder, then headed across the room toward the snacks, walking silently.

LITTLE BREAD
RIDING HOOD

Little Bread Riding Hood—we should probably call her LB, or maybe even Ellbee, for short—was taking a basket of piping hot dinner rolls to her grandmother, who was currently on a fashionable high-carb, low-protein diet that had been made popular by her favorite skinny-as-a-toothpick celebrity spokesperson.

"Be careful in the woods," her mother said as Ellbee headed off.

"I will," Ellbee said, since that was the only acceptable response. Ellbee knew she couldn't reply with something sassy and sarcastic like, "Careful? What fun is that? I plan to gorge myself on highly toxic mushrooms and roll down steep hills covered with poison ivy and sharp rocks. And then I'll rub noses with a rattlesnake and dance the tango with a grizzly bear."

She headed along the familiar path through the woods, enjoying the musical chirps of birds, the gentle touch of the warm breeze, and the tantalizing aroma of hot rolls. When she reached her grandmother's cabin, she knocked on the door.

"Come in," her grandmother called in a hoarse whisper.

"You sound funny," Ellbee said as she opened the door.

"I have a cold," her grandmother said.

"Where are you?" Ellbee asked.

"Up in my bed."

Ellbee went upstairs to her grandmother's bedroom, where she found her grandmother tucked beneath a huge pile of quilts, with her head nestled deep in a stack of fluffy feather pillows.

"Grandma!" Ellbee exclaimed as she noticed the flaring network of scarlet capillaries that ran through the whites of her eyes. "What red eyes you have."

"All the better to see you with, my dear," her grandmother said. She blinked. Then she gasped and wheezed.

"And what wheezy lungs you have," Ellbee said.

"All the better to—uh, wait, let me think—inhale the delicious aroma of the freshly baked rolls," she said.

"And what a pale complexion you have," Ellbee said.

"Uh, all the better to . . ." The words drifted off.

Ellbee realized there was a medical crisis happening. "Too many carbs," she muttered as she tossed the basket of rolls to the floor. She ran outside, hunted down some red meat that was conveniently stalking through the woods not far from the cabin, and made her grandmother a tasty meal of meaty stew.

"Ah, that's better," her grandmother said as she finished her dinner. She reached toward the basket, which was still on the floor. "One roll?"

"Sure," Ellbee said. "Life is all about balance. Just don't overdo it."

"Butter?" her grandmother asked.

Ellbee nodded again. "Not too much." She knew how nice a roll was with a bit of butter.

Right then, the door burst open and the woodcutter raced in, holding his ax high over his head. "Be careful. I heard there's a killer wolf on the prowl."

"Everything is fine. I don't think the wolf is prowling anymore," Ellbee said. "We're just finishing dinner." She pointed toward the kitchen. "Want some stew and a roll?"

"Sure. But just the meat," the woodcutter said. "I'll skip the roll. I'm on a low-carb, high-protein diet, just like my favorite reality show cohost."

Ellbee and her grandmother laughed at that, but they didn't explain to the woodcutter why they found this so amusing.

He'll figure it out sooner or later, Ellbee thought. But she reminded herself to pay the woodcutter a visit the next time she walked through the woods with a basket of rolls for her grandmother, just in case his diet made his eyes too red or his lungs too wheezy. Adults didn't always pay enough attention to what they ate. But Ellbee was always happy to come to the rescue.

GULP

It was really Mom's idea for me to go to the carnival. "You'll have fun," she said. "You'll probably run into lots of your friends."

I didn't bother telling her I couldn't run into lots of friends. She liked to pretend that I was popular. There was no point ruining her fantasy image of me with the truth. And it wasn't as if going to the carnival was some sort of punishment. I'd probably have a good time.

I followed her to the car, took the money she shoved in my hand, and let her drive me across town to the county park, where the Milltown Fire Company annual carnival had set up.

"I'll pick you up at six," Mom called as I walked toward the booths.

I saw people I knew, of course. Lots of them. But nobody who'd be happy if I tried to hang out with him. The first booth I went to had one of those wheels with all the numbers on it.

"Come on, son, try yer luck," the guy running the game said. "It's only a quarter."

I knew it was a long shot. There were a ton of numbers on the wheel. But he was right—it was only a quarter. I studied the board that ran along the front of the booth. *What number?* Didn't really matter. I put the quarter on number twelve, partly because it was right in front of me. Partly because that's how old I was.

A couple other people stepped up and picked numbers. I sort of hoped someone else would also choose twelve, so we could root for it together. Nobody did.

"Good luck," the guy said. He spun the wheel.

It stopped on twelve.

I'd won.

"Here ya go, sport." The guy held out a moldy cardboard box. "You get yer choice."

I looked inside. Candy bars. Old ones with faded wrappers. Ick.

The guy shook the box. "Move it, kid. I ain't got all day. Just pick something. It's all good stuff. Top quality."

I grabbed the closest candy bar. Caramel chews. Even the wrapper felt sticky. I tore it open. There were five shiny brown pieces inside on a cardboard tray. I popped one in my mouth. Then I wrapped the rest of the pieces back up, put them in my pocket.

I don't know why they called them *chews*. Maybe the candy had been chewy ten years ago, but now it was closer to gluey. Once I bit down on the piece in my mouth, it pretty much sealed my teeth together. Though it did taste kind of good. I ground down on it and wriggled my jaw. After a couple minutes, I was actually able to get my teeth unstuck.

I tried to figure out how to kill all the time between now and six, when Mom would pick me up. There were rides. That would be fun. Though I knew that if I rode by myself, people would stare at me. I wandered deeper toward the center of the carnival.

After I finished eating the caramel chew, I realized I was thirsty. There was a booth right ahead of me with old-fashioned sodas. Mom doesn't let me have more than one can a day, so this was a great opportunity. I bought the biggest size they had. I loved root beer. And I loved the idea of drinking as much as I wanted. Before I could take my first sip, someone grabbed my arm, sloshing soda on the ground.

"Thanks. I was dying for a drink."

I looked up. Oh, great. Corbin Malatesta had latched on to me. I was a loner because I had a hard time making friends. He was a loner because he was just too dangerous and mean to hang out with. I let him take the cup from my hand.

He didn't even bother to use a straw. He tilted his head back and chugged my root beer. It was gone in five seconds. I waited for him to burp, but he just grinned and said, "I'm still thirsty. Let's get another."

"But . . ."

He glared at me. I sighed, bought another soda, gave it to him, then tried to slip away. But there was no escape. He put an arm around my shoulder and said, "Now what? I know— let's go on a ride. You'd better buy two tickets. I hate to ride alone, like some kind of loser."

I bought some ride tickets. And then, at Corbin's suggestion, I bought another soda. He gulped that one down, the same way he'd guzzled the other two. I frantically searched for a way to escape. That's when my eyes fell on the Super Scrambler. It was like the old-fashioned Scrambler—four rotating arms, each with four cars on it—but beside spinning, it also shook up and down. As I watched the ride, everything clicked into place, like I was planning out my next three or four moves in a game of checkers.

"That looks kind of scary." I tried my best to sound terrified.

"Perfect. Fear makes me happy." Corbin dragged me toward the Super Scrambler. When we got to the entrance, I gave the guy at the gate two tickets and climbed into one of the cars with Corbin.

Now I had a decision to make. I think every kid reaches a point where he finds out how far he'll go to protect himself. I pulled the pack of caramel chews out of my pocket. It looked like I was about to go pretty far. But I felt good about my choice. I was tired of being a victim.

"There are four," I said. "We can split them."

"I'm not into sharing," Corbin said. "It's me first, me last, and me in the middle." He scooped up all four caramels and popped them in his mouth. I couldn't believe how easy it was to get him to do what I wanted.

As he bit down, the ride started to move. It rotated slowly at first, then built up speed, pressing us against the back of the seat. I heard whoops and shouts from the other riders. Right next to me, I heard something that sounded more like, "Mmmmmuuhhhmmmmm."

Corbin was trying to talk, but his mouth was sealed shut by the caramels. The ride began to jerk up and down in random, violent ways. Corbin's eyes got wider. His cheeks started to puff up. I guess all the soda in his stomach was being shaken pretty heavily.

I was tossed around by the ride, but I couldn't take my eyes off Corbin. I'd seen this old jazz trumpeter on TV once.

When he played, his cheeks puffed out like small balloons. Well, Corbin's cheeks puffed out way more than that. They swelled up bigger and bigger. By now, he was beyond resembling anything human. He reminded me of those frogs who can puff up their necks really far.

His head was thrashing all around, like he was trying hard to unstick his teeth and open his mouth. His cheeks swelled past frog neck, and were moving through water-balloon territory. He clawed at his mouth with both hands. I guess he was trying to pry his jaws open.

The ride jolted so hard, I nearly flew out of my seat. Corbin's eyes got wider, and his whole body shuddered like he'd grabbed an electric eel. Some sort of survival instinct made me duck and close my eyes. It's a good thing. Otherwise, I might have been blinded. As it was, I heard an enormous pop, like when you jump up in the air and come down butt first on a balloon. The pop was followed by a thundering burp that sounded like it would never end.

As the burp finally faded into a moan, and the ride slowed to a drifting stop, I opened my eyes and stared at Corbin. He was sitting straight up now. I think he was in shock. He wasn't moving at all. I looked away when I realized I was seeing the inside of his mouth. His cheeks had exploded, giving me a clear view of the side of his teeth. I unbuckled myself and scooted off the ride.

"I think that kid over there needs a doctor," I said as I ran past the ticket guy. I had a feeling Corbin would need more than one doctor. I also had a feeling it would be a long time before he came back to school.

"Hey—what did you do to Corbin?"

I looked over at Travis Hatcher, who lived down the block

from me. He was standing with Billy Sherman, Jesse Larch, and a couple other kids from school.

"Nothing. He did it to himself," I said.

They all stared over at Corbin.

"He broke my nose last year," Travis said.

"He broke my watch last week," Jesse said.

I started to turn away.

Travis tapped my shoulder. "Come on. You can hang out with us."

"Really?"

"Sure." He pointed toward the drink booth. "We were just about to get a soda. You thirsty?"

I nodded. I realized I was still thirsty. I hoped they had lemonade. Somehow, I wasn't in the mood for anything fizzy.

SPRING BEHIND, FALL AHEAD

It was that stupid nerd Herbert Marlock's fault I was kicked out of school. He was always getting in my face with his wheezy laugh and his look-how-smart-I-am wisecracks. Anybody would have punched him sooner or later. It just happened to be me. It was a good punch, too. Knocked him right off his feet. And knocked me right out of school.

I was halfway home when I realized I had to find a way to fix things. If it was up to me, I'd be happy to stay out of school forever. But my parents told me if I got kicked out again, they'd send me to a military school where they wake you up at five in the morning and make you exercise for an hour and hike ten miles before class. No way I'm doing that.

I knew where Herbert lived. I'd chucked a couple eggs at his house last Halloween after he'd gotten an A on this test I'd flunked. I figured I'd go apologize to his parents for punching their son, and maybe they'd talk to the principal.

I mean, I hadn't broken anything on Herbert's stupid face. Just bruised up his cheek a bit. Maybe I could tell them I'd only hit him because I was jealous about how cool he was. *Gosh, Mr. and Mrs. Marlock, Herbert is totally awesome. I really wish I could be just like him.* Parents eat up that sort of stuff.

I stood on the front steps of the Marlock house and took a couple slow breaths. I needed to look really sorry. And worried. Maybe I could cry a little. That would help—especially with his mom. Women will do anything to stop a kid from crying.

I rang the bell.

A guy answered. He looked like a tall, thin version of Herbert, with a lot less hair.

That could work out okay, too. Most dads want their kids to be tough. Maybe I could convince him I'd be a good role model for Herbert.

"Yes?" He seemed puzzled that someone had rung his doorbell.

"Mr. Marlock?" I asked.

He nodded. But he still seemed like he really wasn't paying attention to me.

"I got in a fight with Herbie at school." That wasn't exactly true. But I rushed through the rest of it as it spilled from my brain to my mouth. "He's okay. Nobody got hurt. It was all my fault. I really wish I could be more like him. I was jealous. He's so awesome. He really knows how to take a punch, too. Anyhow, I wanted to come by, just to tell you how sorry I am."

His mouth twisted around a bit, like he was thinking about everything I'd just told him. Then he smiled. "Okay. Thanks."

He turned away. That's not how this was supposed to go. He was supposed to ask me why I wasn't in school. Then I'd start jerking my shoulders like I was trying not to cry, and tell him I'd been expelled. Yeah, I'd been kicked out of school because Herbie was so awesome.

But he was walking away. He didn't even remember to close the door. The guy was a real geek.

"Wait!"

He turned back toward me. "Yes?"

"I got kicked out of school because of the fight." Oh, no— I'd forgotten to fake the crying part.

"I guess that's the rule."

"Yeah. But I can't get kicked out. My dad's sick. They won't even tell me how sick he is, so it must be pretty bad. And my mom works two jobs because my sister needs an operation, and they can only do it in France because it's really a rare condition."

Wow. I didn't know where all this was coming from, but it was good. It wasn't even totally a lie. My dad had a cold last week. And my mom was always saying that picking up after me was like a full-time job. As for my sister, she needed a brain transplant.

"That's unfortunate," he said.

"It would break their hearts if I got expelled. Do you think, maybe, you could . . ."

I waited, dangling the opening right in front of him.

"Could do what?" he asked.

I wanted to scream. Or punch him. But I managed to stay calm. "Talk to them. At the school. Maybe? Please?"

"I guess I could do that."

I had to struggle to keep from leaping in the air and giving myself a high five. I was saved. No military school.

"Let's go." I needed to get him to talk to the principal before school let out and Herbert showed up. Who knew what that little creep would do to make sure I stayed expelled.

Mr. Marlock glanced at his watch, then did that twisty thing with his lips again. "I just have to wait one more hour. Then we can go."

One hour? School would be out before then. We'd run into Herbert on the way there. "It won't take long," I said.

"I absolutely have to start my next test in—" He paused to glance at his watch. "—fifty-seven minutes. After that, the isotopes will have decayed too far."

He wandered off again. I followed him through the open door and down a hall to the back of the house. We ended up in a room crammed with electronic equipment and tools. Right in the center, there was a chair that looked like it had been yanked out of a sports car. Metal tubes curved around the chair like the ribs of a giant umbrella. I saw wires running from the tubes. One really thick wire ran to the wall, where it was plugged into the big type of socket like they have for clothes dryers.

There was a laptop computer hooked up to the chair, with some large numbers on the screen. The display read +00:15. There was a digital time display above that. I noticed it was fifteen minutes fast. That made me think of school and Herbert. Once he came home, I was doomed. He'd probably start screaming and crying the moment he saw me.

Herbert's dad went to a workbench by the wall and picked up a video camera. When he turned around, he finally seemed to notice me. "I guess it won't be a secret for much longer," he said. "Either I've solved the final problem this time, or it's hopeless."

I had no idea what he was talking about, so I just waited.

He grabbed something that looked like a cordless phone and attached it to the video camera. "I can transmit with this."

"Transmit what?" I asked.

"The arrival." He put the camera down on the seat. "I'm sending it fifteen minutes into the future. I could send it into the past, but it will be more interesting to watch it reappear fifteen minutes from now."

I thought about that for a moment. "You invented a time machine?"

"Somebody had to, eventually. It was only a matter of time." He let out a geeky laugh, like Herbert, and I clasped my hands behind my back to fight the urge to take a swing at him.

He fiddled around at the workbench a bit more and kept talking. There was some sort of problem he was trying to fix. It had something to do with the rotation of the galaxy. I didn't understand it. He used a lot of big words and even bigger numbers. All I understood, as I watched the minutes click past on the laptop, was that Herbert was getting out of school very soon.

No—I understood something else. I didn't need his help. Not if I could get a do-over. I just had to change the setting from +00:15 to –02:00 so I could go back two hours. That would put me in class before I got in trouble. And this time, no matter how tempting it was, I wouldn't hit Herbert.

I slipped over to the computer. As I'd hoped, it was easy enough to change the setting with the mouse. I sat in the chair and flipped the only switch I saw. I heard a low humming sound from underneath the chair. I also heard the front door slam.

"I'm home, Dad."

"Just in time! You can watch the experiment." Herbert's

father took a step toward the door just as the computer let out a beep.

He spun toward me and screamed, "No! I haven't adjusted it for the spatial displacement."

His words were drowned out by a hum that rose to a rumble and then a roar. I felt like my body had been pumped full of seltzer water.

Spatial displacement?

I had no idea what that meant, and no time to wonder. I could swear I was being pulled in every direction at once, and then squished into a tiny ball.

Just when I thought the squishing would get unbearable, I traveled through time. It happened in an eye blink.

I went back two hours.

That's when I understood what Herbert's father meant by *spatial displacement.* I'd gone back two hours. I'd traveled through time. But I hadn't moved from where I was in space.

The earth had moved. It was where it had been two hours ago, leaving me stranded in space. Any kid who's ever watched a science fiction film knows that's a bad thing. As my blood boiled in the vacuum and my flesh froze in the cold, I realized I'd run out of time.

THE GARDEN
OF GARGOYLES

All the kids at Camp Wenaloka knew about the gargoyle garden. A lot of them talked like they'd been there. But Candace suspected most of them were lying. Especially Milly Loftshield, who acted like she was some sort of big deal.

"It's really spooky," Milly said as the girls in the cabin were getting ready to go to sleep. They'd been there just long enough to learn each other's names, but not long enough to establish a leader.

"Can you be more specific?" Candace asked. This was her first year at the camp, so she couldn't even pretend to know about the gargoyles.

"Really, really spooky," Milly said.

Candace snorted. "You've never been there."

"Yes, I have," Milly said.

Candace felt like she was springing a trap. "Then tell us exactly what you saw."

"It was really dark," Milly said. "Really, really dark."

"You're such a liar," Candace said. She could feel the loyalties in the room shifting toward her. She'd be the leader now.

"There were thirteen gargoyles," Milly said. "I counted them as I walked down the path. Each one was more scary than the one before it. They had fangs and wings and horns. Their faces were stretched wide open, like they were screaming."

The room shifted again. Candace hadn't counted on Milly's storytelling skills. The battle might be tougher than she'd expected.

"I thought you told us it was dark," Candace said, trying to regain the advantage.

"I had a flashlight," Milly said.

"So it wasn't dark," Candace said.

"The batteries were weak. The bulb was dim."

Candace saw this wasn't the way to take Milly down. The girl was too crafty. But there was a way to beat her once and for all. "I'm going there right now. And I'm going to count the gargoyles. Then we'll see who really went there."

She forced herself not to grin. It would be so easy to walk off, wait awhile, and then come back and claim she'd counted fifteen gargoyles. She could make up descriptions. That would be easy. She'd had years of practice telling tales, saying whatever she needed to get what she wanted. She headed toward the door.

"How do we know you're really going there?" Milly said. "You could just pretend to go."

Candace's inner grin turned into a snarl. She hadn't expected Milly to figure out her plan. But the game was far from lost. She'd just have to actually go to the gargoyle garden, and take someone with her. "Since you don't trust me,

I'll bring a witness. Who wants to go on an adventure and find out what a liar Milly is?"

The other girls avoided her eyes as Candace glanced around the cabin. She considered the possibilities. Eden was afraid of everything. She'd never go. Lucinda was very smart. Candace considered her a threat. Becky was a possibility. The girl was desperately eager to make friends. Candace knew she could get Becky to do anything. She looked straight at her. "So, who's coming?"

Becky, who was staring at the floor, must have felt Candace's gaze, because she looked up. She gave the tiniest nod. Then she opened her mouth to speak.

Perfect, Candace thought.

"I will," Milly said before Becky could volunteer.

Candace tried to calculate the advantages and disadvantages of accepting the offer. "You could lie about what we see," she said.

Milly held up her phone. "I'll take a picture of each gargoyle. So can you, if you don't trust me. Each of us will have thirteen pictures. You'll see."

Candace could tell this was a bluff. Milly had no idea how many gargoyles there were. She'd never been there. Candace realized Milly expected her to back out. No way.

"Good," Candace said. "Let's go." She grabbed her flashlight and headed out the cabin door, not even waiting to see if Milly followed her. She wanted Milly to have to rush to catch up with her. That would give her even more of an advantage.

"Wait up!" Milly called, keeping her voice at a whisper.

Candace slowed her pace enough for Milly to catch her, but didn't stop. The air was hot and damp. Clouds covered the stars. It wasn't a good night to cross a tree-strewn field, climb a hill, slip past a broken gate, and walk into a garden to count creepy gargoyles.

"We don't have to do this," Candace said. "You just have to admit you've never been there. We can go right back to our beds."

"I told them I'd get pictures," Milly said. "We have to go."

Candace could feel a door closing behind her. Milly was right—there were no options. They couldn't go back to the cabin without visiting the garden. But Candace was sure her victory would be worth the effort, no matter how scary the gargoyles were.

They didn't talk any more during the long walk to the garden, which was on the rear part of the property where a mansion once stood. Nobody had lived there for decades. The large house itself was half collapsed and fully rotted.

The first gargoyle, at the edge of the garden, guarded the entrance to a path lined with hedges. "It's not that scary," Candace said as she took a picture. The gargoyle looked like a cross between a demon and a tiger. "That's one." She walked on.

The second gargoyle, with a face like a bird of prey, was a bit scarier. There was something disturbing about the eyes. They were made of stone, but they looked dangerous and evil.

"Two," Candace said.

The third gargoyle had scary claws. The fourth greeted them with a silent snarl from a terrifying mouth that seemed to drip something wet. Candace didn't look too closely. She kept her eyes on the path ahead, not wanting to stumble across the next gargoyle by surprise.

As they moved closer to the center of the garden, past the

seventh gargoyle, Candace realized she'd won. There was no way there'd be thirteen. Not unless someone had placed a cluster of gargoyles at the end of the path.

"Ready to give up?" she asked Milly.

The girl, slumped in defeat and as silent as the gargoyles, didn't even bother to answer.

In the end, there were only ten gargoyles. The last one, at the center of the garden itself—or what was once a garden back when it had been tended—was by far the scariest, and the largest. It seemed to combine all that was frightening in the other nine, and ramp each horrifying feature up even higher.

"You lied," Candace said.

"Big deal. I've been here now. That's good enough."

"Only because I came," Candace said.

"It doesn't matter. You're new. They won't follow you."

Candace didn't bother arguing. She'd won, and she knew it. She was sure Milly knew it, too. Soon, all the girls would know it. Not just at the cabin, but all through the camp. She'd be the hero, and Milly would be an outcast. What a perfect summer this would be.

As she was about to turn away, she said, "I wonder why anyone would put such ugly creatures in a garden."

"To distract people from the real monster, so you don't notice it's following you."

The words were whispered. Candace glanced to her left. Milly hadn't spoken. Milly's mouth was open, but only because her jaw had started to tremble.

"Did you hear that?" Candace asked.

There was a sigh of evil happiness. It came from behind Candace. The sigh was followed by a shout, in a deep, hoarse rasp. "And now, I will feast on your flesh! *Bwahhh hahhh haaaa!*"

Candace screamed and spun around. A bright light hit her eyes. As her heart slammed against her chest and she struggled to see past the afterimage from the flash, she discovered she was face-to-face with Becky.

"Wow, you really looked scared," Becky said. She clicked two more pictures. "This is perfect. I think you were both at least a foot off the ground in the first picture. And your faces—this is priceless." She turned and dashed off.

"We're doomed," Candace said.

"It's your fault," Milly said.

"You're the one who lied," Candace said.

"You're the one who wanted to make me look bad."

"Only because you lied."

"You started it."

"No, I didn't."

They argued all the way back. It was a long, slow walk. Candace knew that neither of them was eager to return to the cabin, or to the camp, where Becky—sly, sneaky Becky— would rule over both of them for the rest of the summer.

ALIEN BIOLOGY

Xlatspan isn't difficult. Or maybe I just have a knack for alien languages. Out of all the kids at Damon Knight Middle School, I'm the best in my class at speaking it, which is why my teacher told me I should apply for a chance to be an exchange student.

So I went online and filled out all the forms. And I got accepted. I'll be spending a whole marking period on the nearest planet colonized by the Xlatspanzy.

I'm on the ship now. It only takes two weeks—336 Earth hours—to get there, even though it's a couple dozen light-years away. I don't understand that part. Not yet. But one of the classes I'll be taking is called Muon Drive Physics. Actually, it's called *K'etch chzwad metma metmo*. That's how they say it.

I'm also taking History of the Xlatspanzy Empire, Alien Biology, and Contemporary Art Forms. I've already seen some amazing art, both from the Xlatspanzy and from some of the other races they've met in their explorations.

The Xlatspanzy are sort of scary when you first meet them.

They're shorter than the average human, but pretty strong looking. Their heads are big. Not enormous, like aliens in movies, but big enough that you know they aren't human. I've heard they have two hearts. I guess I'll learn all about that in the biology class.

It's great that I get to practice the language all the time. It works both ways. As much as I like to practice my Xlatspan, that's how much they like to practice their English. About half the crew members on the ship are learning to speak it. Some of them are pretty good, though all of them have trouble with the V sound, since their lips work differently from ours.

Almost exactly two weeks after we left Earth, a light started to flash from the ceilings and walls. That meant we were about to emerge from non-space and transition into landing orbit. I slid inside one of the cushioned tubes in the common room. The landing was pretty rough, but I was prepared. They'd warned us we'd feel some jolts and a brief period of high gravity.

There were a couple hundred other kids on the ship, from all over the world, but I didn't hang out with them much. Most of them were pretty stuck up. It didn't matter. Only one of us would go to each school, so it wasn't like I'd have any friends where I was going. And I was a lot more interested in getting to know the Xlatspanzy.

I'd be staying with an actual family. That was great. Their homes are nothing like ours. But I'd been told they'd made up a room for me with a bed and everything.

I started my classes the next day. I had to admit, the physics class was pretty tough. As good as I was at the language, it was hard understanding all that science information when it was spoken in Xlatspan.

Art was great. The instructor even showed a piece from Earth. As she talked about it and tried to pronounce *van Gogh*, all my classmates glanced at me, then looked away. I guess they were shy.

After art, we headed to Alien Biology. The desks were in a circle around a large table with straps. When I walked in, everyone stared at me.

I said hello in Xlatspan.

Nobody answered me. Someone grabbed me from behind. Then a couple more of them grabbed me. They lifted me up and put me on the table. I tried to get away, but straps shot across my arms, legs, and chest.

I couldn't move. But I could hear.

"Welcome to Alien Biology," the instructor said. "We are fortunate to finally have a live specimen. We'll go slowly and carefully, since he has to last the whole marking period."

The teacher picked up some sort of shiny tool and walked toward me. "The skin is composed of three layers."

I screamed and begged for them to let me go. In English. Not that it mattered.

EVIL IS IN THE EYE
OF THE BEHOLDER

My grandparents are in Greece," I said. "They're traveling all over Europe this month. They'll be in Turkey next."

You'd think I'd made the announcement in Greek. For a moment, nobody even looked up. Then Sarah McEdmonds put down her Brie-with-dried-cranberries sandwich and said, "We're summering in Paris."

"So are we," Lydea Betterson said. "After we leave London. I do so love European capitals."

The other five girls at our lunch table started talking about their next vacation. They were hitting all the continents except for Antarctica, and most of the places I'd dreamed about seeing someday—Paris, Rome, Madrid, Singapore. I went back to eating.

I shouldn't have said anything about my grandparents' trip. I definitely shouldn't have tried to impress the girls at the table.

I'll never learn, I thought. I was at Holidale Prep on a scholarship. My parents weren't poor, but they worked hard just to keep ahead of the bills, and could never have afforded private school without help. My grandparents worked hard, too. They might be in Europe right now, but they definitely hadn't flown there first-class, and they sure weren't staying at fancy hotels or eating expensive meals.

"So, Meredith," Sarah said to me after she'd finished her sandwich, "where are you going this summer?"

I shrugged. "Don't know yet." She'd hardly be impressed with our plans to spend a week camping in the Adirondacks. I loved everything about those mountains—the blue skies, the flocks of birds, the smell of pine trees—but none of the girls at the table would understand.

"Oh, it must be wonderful to be so spontaneous," Sarah said. "I imagine you could fly off anywhere. Maybe Ipanema, or Dubai. I hope you'll send me a postcard."

"I'll try to remember." I had no idea where either of those places was, but I knew they were out of reach. I turned my attention to my fruit cup, which I'd saved for dessert. I still couldn't decide whether Sarah was mean, evil, or merely clueless. I was leaning toward 80 percent clueless, with a dash of mean and a pinch of evil.

I did get to go to the airport before the start of summer, but not to take a trip. At the end of the month, my whole family— Mom, Dad, my older sister, and my younger brother—drove there on a Friday night to pick up Grammy and Gramps.

They looked great. Gramps scooped me up and swung me around. He's a lot younger than my friends' grandfathers, and he takes really good care of himself. When he was in college, he was on the wrestling team.

"I brought you a surprise," he whispered.

But he made me wait until we got home to see it. Finally, when we were all gathered in the living room, he held out a small cloth pouch that Grammy took from her carry-on bag.

"Reach in," he said.

I reached in and felt something small, smooth, hard, and cool. I pulled it out. "It's beautiful." The stone looked sort of like colored glass. It was flat and round, maybe four inches wide, with circles on it, like a bull's-eye. Except, instead of red and white, it was white, light blue, and dark blue.

I could feel my brow wrinkle as I tried to figure out what I had in my hand. It was pretty, but I was sure there had to be more to the present than that. "What is it?"

"It's a good luck charm," he said.

"What kind of luck?" I asked.

"It protects you from the evil eye," he said.

I was learning less with each answer. "Evil eye?"

Gramps nodded. "Everyone in Turkey owns one. They feel it protects you from the sort of harm that comes from envy. People who envy you often wish for bad things to happen. Get rid of the envy, and you get rid of the danger."

"Thanks." I gave him a hug. I loved the way the charm looked. But as I was taking it with me to my bedroom that night, I thought about the evil eye. Nobody envied me. I had nothing to worry about in that area.

But I had another thought. The next day, I looked online and found a store in town that sold good luck charms. Luckily, they weren't really expensive, so I was able to buy as many as I needed. Monday, I took them to school with me.

"I have presents for all of you," I said at lunch.

That got their attention.

"What is it?" Sarah asked.

I reached into my purse and pulled out the five wrapped good luck charms. "See for yourself." I passed them out.

Sarah and the others unwrapped the presents. I thought they'd be puzzled, but Lydea nodded and said, "How nice. I've seen these in Ankara."

The other girls also knew what they were. But they took them. And I knew they'd keep them. Which was all I wanted. Now, Sarah, Lydea, and the rest of the girls at my table would be safe from envy. Specifically, they'd be protected from my envy.

They are all going to Europe for the summer. They are rich, and they get whatever they want. They'll always have more things than I'll have. After I repeated those thoughts several times, I searched my mind for signs of envy.

Nothing.

I was fine with that. They had their lives, and I had mine. I had my family. I had our week in the Adirondacks. I had Grammy and Gramps. I didn't envy their good fortune. I had no desire to give them the evil eye.

The charms worked beautifully.

THE DARK SIDE
OF BRIGHTNESS

I **want a dazzling** smile!" Cranston screamed.

His parents exchanged puzzled glances and then turned nervous smiles in his direction.

"What was that?" his mother asked.

"A dazzling smile," Cranston said. "Didn't you hear me the first time?"

"We did," his father said. "But we aren't sure what you mean. Your smile is just wonderful."

"It's not dazzling." Cranston pointed toward the closest television, which was currently tuned to a channel featuring entertainment news. "In the ads, the beautiful people have dazzling smiles."

Cranston, who was eight years old, watched far too much television, which wasn't difficult, since there was a set in nearly every room in the house. Some celebrities could sing or dance. Others could act or tell jokes. Some didn't seem to have any talent at all. But they all had dazzling smiles. Every single one of them. Cranston was pretty sure he didn't have any talent, so his only hope of being a celebrity was his smile.

"Your smile is already perfect," his mother said. She took his chin in her hand and told him, "You're my perfect little angel, and your smile is just right."

Cranston issued a howl of frustration and stomped out of the room. Nobody seemed to understand how important this was. He needed a dazzling smile, and he needed it right now. His neighbor's mother was a celebrity. Becky's mom gave the weather forecast on the local news channel, and appeared in commercials for a used-car dealer. On the news and in the commercials, her smile was dazzling. Whenever she had to go anywhere, a limousine picked her up. Whenever she went into town, people asked her for her autograph. That's what happened when you had a dazzling smile.

Cranston knocked on Becky's door.

"Hi?" she said. Cranston never talked to her, and had never knocked on her door before, so she was puzzled by his sudden appearance.

"I want a dazzling smile," he told her.

"No problem," Becky said. "My mom uses these strips. They make her teeth totally dazzling. I use them, too."

Becky flashed a stunning grin at Cranston. He almost asked her for her autograph, but he had more urgent things to do. Becky led him to her parents' bathroom and opened the cabinet under the sink. There were seven boxes of Perfect-Smile Concentrated Whitening Strips stacked on the bottom shelf.

"Can I have one?" Cranston asked.

"Sure." Becky reached inside an open box for a strip.

"No. Not one strip. One box," Cranston said. He was pretty sure one strip wouldn't do the trick. If it did, why would anyone need seven boxes?

Becky shrugged and handed him a full box. "Here you go."

"Thanks." Cranston carried the box back home and went up to his bedroom. He read the first line of the directions on the side of the box. *Place strip against teeth and let sit for fifteen minutes.*

Cranston didn't bother reading the rest. He took out the strip, placed it against his teeth, and checked the clock on his desk. The strip tasted like glue mixed with mouthwash. Cranston didn't care. He'd do anything for a dazzling smile.

After fifteen minutes, he took off the strip and flashed a grin toward his mirror.

The grin had a short life.

"They're the same!" he screamed. He leaned so close to the mirror that his breath fogged it. As far as he could tell, his smile still wasn't dazzling.

He put on another strip and left it there for two minutes. Then he took it off and grabbed a fresh one.

By the tenth strip, he was pretty sure he was seeing a change. He kept it up until the box was empty. That's when he noticed the line below the instructions that warned: *Do not use more than two strips each day.*

A moment later, his mom walked into the room. She glanced down at the scattered litter of thirty wrappers and thirty used whitening strips. "What are you doing?"

Instead of answering, Cranston decided to show her. He gave her his most dazzling smile. He knew, when she saw it, she'd let him do whatever he wanted. That was the power of a dazzling smile.

His mom gasped, put her hand over her mouth like she was holding back a scream, and staggered away until she bumped into a wall across the hall from the bedroom door.

Cranston was about to ask her what was wrong, when he

realized his legs felt strange. Something had spilled on them. It looked like little splashes of sour cream. He felt more wetness on his chin, and on the front of his shirt.

I'm drooling?

"What . . ."

As he spoke, he realized his tongue was striking emptiness. Cranston stared at his face in the mirror. He definitely didn't have a dazzling smile. Far from it. His teeth were gone. They'd dissolved into a liquid and dribbled out of his mouth.

It was a bright, dazzling liquid, but it would never be part of another smile.

DAY CARELESS

Jordan, I need you to pick up Danube," my mom called as she rushed toward the garage with my baby brother Nile tucked in one arm and a diaper bag dangling from the other.

"What?" I hit START on the controller to bring up the PAUSE screen and looked over at her from the couch.

"Pick up your brother from day care. I have to take Nile for his booster shot."

"But . . ." I pointed at the screen. Clearly, I was nowhere near a save spot. It had taken me fifteen minutes to fight my way to where I was, and I didn't want to face the poison-spitting giant cockroaches again. No thanks. They were just too hard to kill. I'd barely made it past them this time. As it was, my health bar was nearly gone.

"No argument," Mom said. "It's just a couple blocks away. Three-fifty-nine Burlman Street. Go there. Get him. Walk him home. Then you can get back to your game. Under-stand?" She vanished into the garage before I even had a chance to nod.

I left the game paused and headed out the front door. Burl-man Street was more than a couple blocks away. A *couple* meant "two." Not seven. But there was nobody I could complain to. And even if there were, it wouldn't do me any good.

When I reached the place, I saw that it wasn't a building. It was someone's house. But I spotted a hand-painted sign in front: DAY CARE. CHEAP RATES.

As I walked up to the front door, I could hear the squealy noise of little kids coming from inside. Danube is four, which makes him close to useless as far as the two of us having fun together. I can make him do stupid things, but that gets boring pretty quickly.

I knocked on the door and waited. Nobody came. I knocked again. I waited awhile longer, and then really thumped it. Finally, the door opened and a woman peeked out. She looked like she was maybe forty or fifty years old. I could tell she was having a rough day. Her hair was all messy, like someone had tossed a small bomb onto her head. Her dress was rumpled. She smelled like meat loaf—but not the good kind my grandma makes. More like the kind they serve at school.

"Yes?" she asked.

"I'm here to pick up Danube," I said.

"Who?"

"Danube. My brother." I lowered my hand like I was patting the top of his head. "Little guy. Runny nose. Brown hair. Likes trucks."

"Oh, sure. Come in." She led me through a living room, where the TV was on. A steaming cup of tea rested on a table next to a large chair. I didn't see any sign of kids, but I could hear them. The woman opened a door on the wall next to the table. The squeals got louder. I followed her downstairs to a basement. I spotted Danube over in one corner, playing with some wooden blocks. Other kids were playing with cheap toys, watching a cartoon video on an ancient TV, or just sitting doing nothing.

Before I could call for Danube, the woman said, "Look. I need a favor. I have to run out for five minutes to pick up my prescription. Can you watch them?"

I glanced at the room full of toddlers, ranging from babies to a couple kids who were older than Danube. "No way."

She reached in her pocket and pulled out some money. "Five dollars for five minutes," she said.

"Ten."

"Deal."

She shoved a bill in my hand and left, closing the door at the top of the stairs.

"Jordan!"

Danube had spotted me. He rushed over and gave me a sticky hug. Mom and Dad had named us all after rivers, which is pretty funny when you think about how dirty Danube and Nile get. It's sort of crappy for me, since Jordan could also be a girl's name. Luckily, I'm a pretty good fighter. Even if I did have a hard time getting past the giant cockroaches.

"Home?" Danube asked.

"Soon. We just have to hang out here for a few minutes."

Above, I heard the sound of the front door closing. The slam was followed by no sound at all. It took me a second or two to realize the squealing and chattering had turned into silence. The kids in the room had stopped babbling at each other or crying or screaming. Every single one of them was staring at me.

I took Danube's sticky hand and walked up the steps. I figured I'd wait in the kitchen, right near the door to the basement, until I heard the woman coming back, and then slip down here again so she wouldn't know what I'd done. It would only be a couple minutes. Nothing bad would happen to the kids in that little bit of time. And as far as I remembered, she didn't say I had to stay in the same room with them. *Watch the kids* doesn't mean I had to actually look at them.

"Home?" Danube asked again. He clutched my pants leg in one fist and squeezed it like he was trying to extract khaki juice. His other fist remained locked onto my hand.

"Soon." It was still creepily silent behind me. I grabbed the knob and turned it. My gut clenched as I realized the door was locked.

I pushed hard, but the door was too solid for me to force open. "Okay," I said out loud, "it's no big deal. She just wants to keep us safe. She'll be back in a minute. Right?" I asked, as if Danube could answer questions that required real thought.

"Right," he said.

I looked past the stairs to the basement floor. "You want to wait down there with your friends?"

"No." He shook his head hard.

I couldn't blame him. "Okay. We'll stay here."

Down below, the kids had gotten to their feet. All of them. They moved to the bottom of the stairs. They still hadn't made a sound.

One of them, barely older than a baby, crawled up to the second step. He looked at me and opened his mouth. I expected some sort of babbling baby sounds. Instead, I heard words.

"Big people are bad." His voice was like an old man's whisper. A girl about Danube's age pointed at me. "You're big."

"You're bad," the baby said.

They all pointed at me. "You're bad!" they cried.

"No!" I screamed.

Next to me, Danube howled. I thought he was just scared. Then he howled louder and yanked at my hand. I looked down. I was so scared, I was squeezing his hand. Hard.

I let go.

"Bad!"

They swarmed up the stairs. I scanned around for any way to escape. There was no other way out. I hit the door with my shoulder, but it didn't budge.

The baby had reached me. I raised my hand to push him back down. But I hesitated. How could I push a baby?

In the brief time when I'd paused, two more of them reached my step. They clutched at my pants legs. I tried to push one of them off. The baby grabbed my arm.

They swarmed over me, like ants on a scrap of meat. They pulled at my legs and tugged at my belt. When I realized I was in trouble, I pushed Danube away so he wouldn't fall with me. I toppled, rolling down the steps. As I tumbled, I caught sight of him tottering at the top of the steps. Luckily, he managed to keep his balance.

The rest of the kids fell with me. On the way down, I had the weirdest thought. I was like a *katamari* in that old video game, a sticky ball picking up everything I rolled over.

I crashed to a stop against a ratty old stuffed giraffe, still mobbed by the kids. They were pummeling me. None of them could hit all that hard, but I was at the center of a lot of fists and feet.

I had a difficult time breathing with so many kids piled on my chest. My head hurt. So did my ribs. The room started to get dark in a weird way, like someone had pulled a piece of red silk across my eyes.

They're killing me.

It was strange. Part of my brain didn't seem to mind. The other part told me to struggle.

The door at the top of the steps opened. Light washed over me.

"I'm back."

Kids fell from me and scrambled to the corners of the room. They acted like they'd never left their games or toys.

I stood and took a deep breath, then headed up the steps. I forced myself not to run. When I got to the top, I took Danube's hand. Gently. I was definitely happy when we made it through the kitchen and out the front door. On the way out, I noticed a bag on the kitchen table. It wasn't from the drugstore. It was from the doughnut shop. She'd gone away and left all those kids with someone who really wasn't qualified to watch them, all for a snack.

"Home?" Danube asked as we walked toward the street.

"Yeah."

"I don't like that place," he said.

I patted his shoulder. "Don't worry. You're never going back there."

Maybe none of those kids is going back, I thought. Not after I told Mom what happened. Those kids might have acted like monsters, but I didn't think they were born that way. Someone, or something, had made them act like that.

We reached our house. I could finally get back to my game

and finish the level. As I picked up the controller, Danube tugged at my sleeve.

"Play my game?" he asked.

I almost shouted at him to go away. But the image of those kids froze my anger. "Sure. I'll tell you what. I just need a couple minutes. Go get yourself a juice box, and then we'll play."

"Yay!" He raced out of the room.

I finished the level, saved my game, and loaded up his. For a kiddie game, it wasn't all that bad. I was glad about that. I had a feeling I'd be spending a lot more time with Danube from now on. But I think that's a good thing. A very good thing.

RAT SLAYERS

My luck is holding, Alarac thought as his blade sliced clear through the neck of the giant rat. That was an unlikely stroke with a single-handed sword, but he'd felt confident enough to risk one powerful blow rather than try to wear his opponent down with a flurry of slashes and jabs.

"Well fought," the barbarian Golgetha cried as he swung his own twin-bladed battle-ax in a wide arc, dealing vast damage to three more rats that he'd backed into a corner of the cellar. "You are becoming a capable warrior."

"I'm honored by your words." Alarac hoped he'd soon be strong enough to wield a two-handed sword, or maybe even a pike. The idea of striking at his foes from a distance appealed to him, though his skills lay more in the area of blades than spears. Too bad he had no talent at all for bows and arrows.

He dashed forward to help Golgetha finish off the three wounded rats. The task didn't take long.

"Onward?" he asked, turning toward the door that led to the next area of the mazelike cellar beneath the flour mill.

"Always." Golgetha let out a laugh and flung open the door.

They rushed through. It was dark, but Alarac used the one weak spell he knew to light the torches on the walls. The light, reflected in two dozen pairs of red eyes, revealed more enemies awaiting them.

"The mill owner will be paying us well," he said as he moved to his left. They'd been promised a bounty of six copper pieces for each rat they slew.

Working together, Alarac and Golgetha made short work of the rats. Another door lay ahead. Alarac sensed that a more dangerous foe lurked on the other side. As he moved toward the door, he spotted something hidden amongst the shadows near a pile of old barrels.

"A club," he said. There it lay, abandoned atop a scattered assortment of bones. "I suppose it didn't do much good for the former owner." He picked up the club and felt the weight in his hand. He could definitely wield it. He had enough strength. It wasn't his customary weapon—he'd done all his fighting with a blade—but he couldn't help himself. He had to test it against the rats. He slid his sword into the scabbard on his back and prepared to battle the next enemy with the help of the club.

"Are you sure?" Golgetha asked.

"I am."

They pushed on through the door, where the hulking sight of an enormous rat greeted them. It was so large, its back brushed the ceiling, and its whiskers were as thick as fingers. Alarac thought about retreating, but the door slammed shut behind him.

The rat leaped forward. There was no time to switch

weapons. Alarac rushed to meet it, swinging the club. He struck the rat on its massive flank with a clumsy blow, doing no damage at all. The club was trickier to use than he'd realized. Alarac wondered whether he should risk reaching for his sword. Before he could decide, the rat lashed out with alarming speed, snapping its jaws down on his shoulder.

The club fell to the floor. Alarac screamed as his severed arm also fell. Alarac knew his health was draining rapidly. The pain was unbearable. He tried to grab medicine from the pouch at his belt with his remaining hand. He could save his life if he hurried. Golgetha was too busy defending himself from the rat to come to Alarac's aid. But the pouch was crammed with an assortment of small vials and flasks, only one of which would heal large wounds.

Alarac fell, his health completely gone. As he faded away, he saw the rat lash out again. It clamped its jaws down on Golgetha's body, catching him at the waist. The rat lifted Golgetha from the ground and flung him against the wall.

As Golgetha faded, a message expanded to fill the middle of the screen. GAME OVER. RETRY FROM LAST CHECKPOINT?

Quentin threw down the controller and turned toward Luke. "What was that nonsense with the club? Why in the world would you use a club against a boss? You spent hours raising your sword stats. What were you thinking?"

Luke shrugged. "I don't know. I just felt like trying it. I had no idea the boss would be that tough. No big deal. It's a fun level. I don't mind replaying from the last save. It's not that far from where we died."

"Okay, but stick with the sword this time."

"Whatever." Luke hit X.

Alarac unsheathed his sword as he emerged from the well of memories. Four rats lay ahead of him—three toward the right side, and a single creature to the left. "I'll take that one," he said.

Golgetha raised his ax and charged toward the three rats. Alarac attacked his single foe. He decided to try for a critical blow, swinging right for the neck. *Maybe I'll get lucky*, he thought.

FRIGID REGULATIONS

There are several rules every girl who lives up here learns as soon as she's old enough to walk. Boys learn them, too, but you know how boys are when it comes to rules. They like to take risks and show off, which is why a lot of them get hurt. Especially around here, where any mistake might be your last. I think rule number two is the one they violate the most. But here are all of them:

1. Always wear a cross when going outside.
2. Don't go outside alone.
3. Never invite a stranger into your home.
4. Don't forget to rub garlic on your neck.
5. Wash your hands before eating.

I'm pretty sure my mom added the fifth rule, because lots of my friends never wash their hands before eating. Besides, I don't see how clean hands can protect you from vampires. But I always pay attention to the first four rules, because I really don't want to get drained of all my blood and turned into one of the undead. And it's not like we have to worry about it all year long. The rules are really just for the dark period, when the sun never peeks over the horizon. But I don't mind. It's so beautiful up here, far to the north of all the rest of the country, that I'd never want to live anywhere else. You just have to respect the weather, and remember the dangers.

The problem is, vampires might be undead, and cold-blooded, and centuries old, but there's one way they're a lot like us—they get tired of the same old routine. They love to go on vacation. We get flooded with vampires during the dark period, when they aren't in danger of being crisped by the sun.

Every year at this time, they're all over the place. They try to act like they're just regular people. Two or three years ago, I found a booklet that one of them had accidentally left behind, with tips for blending in with the residents. It explained stuff like how to dress as if you could feel the cold, and how to talk about local issues. But as hard as they try to avoid notice, they don't fool us. You can spot one easily enough. Luckily, for the most part, they behave themselves, since they don't want us to get so annoyed that we start hunting them down. But they aren't always able to resist temptation, which is why the rules are so important.

On the positive side, they spend a lot of money here, which is good for the economy. So we deal with the annual invasion. We wear crosses, rub ourselves with garlic, and make sure never to invite a stranger inside. Because it's true—a vampire can't enter your house without permission.

It was a Saturday afternoon, right near the end of the dark period. My parents had gone off to the store for groceries. I'd decided to wash my hair. The colder it gets outside, the more I appreciate hot water. But I still didn't want to get myself totally wet. So I bent over the sink in the kitchen and used the sprayer to soak my head.

I have great hair. I'm not bragging. It's a fact. Mom has great hair, too, so I guess I got it from her. After I worked up the lather, I started playing around. I guess I was just as bored as the vampires. First, I made myself look like a punker with a mohawk. I snarled at my reflection in the side of the toaster, trying to act like a rock star with a bad attitude.

Then I swirled my hair into two buns, like Princess Leia in the old *Star Wars* movie. I'd just started turning my head into the Statue of Liberty's crown when the doorbell rang.

Oh, great.

Statue of Liberty is a totally secret game I've never told anyone about. Not even my best friend. I make spikes in my hair that look just like Lady Liberty's crown. Then I stand there with a towel draped around my shoulders like a robe and welcome immigrants to America. I make up stories about their struggles and about the good fortune they'll find in the land of the free. Sometimes I tuck a book under my arm. But the books get wet if I'm not careful, so I don't do that very often.

The doorbell rang again.

I was tempted to ignore it. But it could be my parents. Dad had a habit of forgetting stuff, including his house key. Maybe he'd come back for it. It was about twenty degrees below zero outside, so I knew he and Mom wouldn't appreciate waiting.

I draped a towel around my shoulders and went down the hall to the entryway. There's no glass in the front door, so I had to open it.

It wasn't my parents. It was that annoying boy, Barton Holdrup, from down the street. He was standing on the front porch, shivering.

"What?" I asked.

"My house is on fire. I need to use your phone."

That was terrible. Fires were one of the worst things that could happen when it got really cold. It's hard to spray water when everything freezes so quickly. "Come in!" I stepped back and opened the door.

As Barton walked inside, three thoughts hit me all at once. First, I didn't smell smoke. The air here is so crisp and clean, any smell stands out. Barton's house was less than a quarter mile down the road. Second, Barton always has his cell phone with him. We all do. Even if he didn't, he'd probably risk getting burned to grab it before he ran out of the house. We all would. Third, he was looking pretty pale.

Barton smiled, and revealed his fangs.

I might not have totally broken rule number three when I invited him in—he wasn't really a stranger—but he'd obviously stopped being Barton. I had a feeling his transformation had happened very recently. He was probably hunting for his first blood. But this was no time to think things over, since it was obvious he wanted that first blood to come from me.

I had to get away.

Vampires are fast. Not as fast as in the movies, but faster than anyone would like them to be. He probably expected me to run into the house and try to hide, or block off my bedroom door while I called for help. I was pretty sure that would be a bad move. Vampires are also strong. Not as strong as in the movies, but definitely strong enough to break down a door.

I couldn't outrun or outfight him. I needed to outsmart him. That should be possible. It was Barton, after all. He was stronger and faster, now that he was one of the undead, but he wasn't any smarter.

Instead of zigging toward the hallway, I zagged right out the front door.

The bitter cold air slashed at the exposed skin of my face and hands. I could feel the damp towel start to freeze around my neck. Too bad that wouldn't be enough to stop a vampire's bite. He'd tear through the cloth like a wolf through a rabbit.

I ran, not risking the time it would take to look back. I heard footsteps behind me, crunching on the snow. Good. At least he hadn't been a vampire long enough to learn how to skim the ground.

Where to go? The nearest house was thirty yards down the road. I'd never reach it before he caught me. The garage was no good. If I went there, I'd be trapped inside, without any place to hide. Suddenly, leaving the house seemed like the worst idea of my life.

The footsteps got closer. The air bit at me like a million piranhas made of ice. Each breath I took stabbed into my lungs like a dagger, or a sharp stake.

Stake!

That was my only chance. And it wasn't going to be fun.

I slid to a stop and spun around to face Barton. He was racing toward me with his mouth wide open. I screamed and held up my hands, like I was trying to stop him.

He leaped at me, arms spread to grab my shoulders.

Here goes. I was about to risk my neck.

I bent over just enough to put my head at the same level as his chest. He slammed into me. Two screams ripped the air as I got knocked back by the impact.

I screamed in terror, and also disgust, as I felt a spike of frozen hair on top of my head sink into Barton's body. He screamed because one of the few things that hurts a vampire is a stake through the heart. Or, in my case, a frozen spike. At least my neck didn't snap.

Now I had a problem. To kill a vampire, you have to leave the stake in his heart and then cut his head off. I wasn't really eager to do either of those things. So I was stuck. Literally. And so was Barton. A real stake would have paralyzed him, but it looked like frozen hair was good enough to slow him down.

I took a step forward, pushing at him. He took a step backward, offering no resistance. He was howling a bit, but not as loudly as before. Staying bent over, I walked all the way to my house. Then I turned him around and backed up, keeping my fists clenched on his shirt so I could pull him along. It felt weirdly like we were dancing.

When I reached the door, I said, "Barton, I take back my permission. You can't enter my house." I wasn't sure whether that would work, but I couldn't think of anything else to try. I groped behind myself until I felt the edge of the open door. I grabbed it with one hand and put the other against his chest. Then I gave a hard push.

Barton toppled backward, sliding free of the spike. I wasn't sure what would happen next. I got ready to slam the door and make a run for my cross and garlic.

Barton lay where he'd fallen, clutching his chest. "Man, that hurt."

"Are you coming after me?" I asked.

. He shook his head. "I can't. You took back the permission."

I was glad to hear my idea had worked. "How'd it happen?"

He shrugged. "I broke a couple of the rules. I wanted to hang out with the vampires. They're so awesome. I figured I'd be okay. My mistake." He got to his feet. "Well, I guess I'd better head out of here. It's not going to be dark all that much longer."

"Bye . . .," I said.

"Bye. Sorry about trying to drain your blood. I'm new at this." He gave me a little wave. "See you next year."

Next year? Oh, great. I had a feeling I needed to start paying more attention to the rules. Or washing my hair every night. I thought about telling Mom she needed to change rule number five. Clean hands wouldn't have saved my life. But I decided it was better not to tell her anything at all.

DOG GONE

I t is a tedious process, but one I only need to perform three or four times a year. People might think I'd need to do it far more often, but people are wrong about that. People are wrong about many things. That's good. It helps me stay safe.

Three and a half months have passed since the last time. So the moment has come. First, I have to find the house.

That part takes the longest. The house needs to be just right. It has to be unoccupied, of course. I could select a house with a single occupant, but that would lead to an investigation, since people notice these things when a home owner is involved. And the whole point of this exercise is to avoid notice. I always try to avoid making any sort of waves. I'm very good at that. I've had many years of practice.

So I went house hunting. After three days, I found the perfect place. It was on a quiet street, with no house directly opposite it. The houses on either side were separated from it by rows of dense evergreens. I am quite fond of the blue spruce. It blocks light and absorbs sound.

Next, I needed the dog. That was the easy part. But not as

easy as it might seem. I required one that was friendly and approachable. Small, but not too small. The very small dogs tend to cower and hide.

I found a stray running loose in the city. He looked to be part sheltie. I fed him and petted him. He licked my hand. Good. He'd be perfect.

Last, I made tags for his collar. I have a machine for that. It's just a mechanical press with movable letters. It takes a while to set up the words, since each letter has to be placed in a slot by hand, but I'm patient. Very patient.

"What shall we call you?" I asked as I sorted through the small letters in the tray. "Spot? Rover?"

He stared at me, tongue out, nose moist, eyes alert.

"No. Something cuter," I said. "I have it. You shall be *Scooter*. How adorable."

I plucked the necessary letters from the tray and set them in the first line of the press. I placed the address of the house in the next two lines. I stamped the tag and then attached it to the collar I'd bought the other day.

That evening, I dropped Scooter off a half dozen blocks away. Then I returned to the house and waited.

Sometimes it takes hours. If it grew too late, I'd go find Scooter and try again the next evening. This time, the doorbell rang less than half an hour after I got back.

A boy stood on the porch, with Scooter cradled in one arm. "Mister, is this your dog?" he asked.

I smiled at him, but made sure not to open my mouth. My fangs were already growing. The thought of a meal was enough to make them spring forth. I was hungry, and eager to feed. My veins and arteries hummed in anticipation.

I stepped back. He stepped forward. I led him inside. He

had no idea what was about to happen. There was no hint of fear in his eyes or heart. That was good. I'm not fond of the smell of fear, or the taste it leaves behind.

Once he was fully inside, I seized him and drank his blood. I was quick and merciful. He didn't suffer. Then I hid the body deep in the woods, where it would never be found. I'm very good at that, too.

I went back to the house to pick up Scooter, of course. I had already made sure to find a good home for him, in a loving family with two young children. There was no way I'd abandon the poor dog. It's not like I'm some sort of monster.

A WORD OR TWO ABOUT THESE STORIES

As always, I'll wrap things up by revealing how I got the idea for each of these stories. Be warned—there are many spoilers here.

Playing Solo

After playing a marathon session of the original *Gears of War*, I imagined a kid who was so wrapped up in a game that he didn't notice what was happening in the real world. (I'll admit I often get totally absorbed in playing games or reading books. Sometimes I even get swallowed up by writing stories.) There's added irony when the events in the world—in this case, an alien invasion—are similar to those of the game.

Gorgonzola

When I visit schools, I'm often asked, "What's your favorite cheese?" (I'm also asked about my favorite pie.) I guess people expect an answer like "American" or "cheddar." But my taste in cheeses runs similar to my taste in roller coasters and short stories. I like extreme ones—the sort that strike terror in the majority of folks. I like runny, stinky, horrifying cheeses. So it's not unusual to have some Stilton or Gorgonzola in the fridge. I was looking at a label one day, and it hit me that *Gorgonzola* contained *Gorgon*. (I like wordplay even more than cheese.) It was easy to go from there to thinking how Gorgons could make Gorgonzola. (As for pie—sour cherry.)

Blowout
As faithful Weenies fans know, one of my main sources of inspiration is my "what-if" file. I start each workday by writing a question. Then, when I'm looking for an idea, I scan through the file, hoping one of the entries will intrigue me or spawn further thoughts. (The "what-if" itself is just a scaffold or a seed. I need to build on it or let it grow to have a full story.) In this case, the question was, *What if a kid could blow out stars?* I loved the image of stars blinking out. I loved the image even more when I realized the closest star wouldn't be immune to the magic.

Christmas Carol
The title inspired the story. I'm not sure why, but my mind likes to take common phrases and find new meanings in them. Sometimes, as in this case, the phrase is left intact. Other times, as in the story "The La Brea Toy Pits" (from an earlier collection) or "Little Bread Riding Hood," the words get twisted into a pun. From there, it became a "be careful what you wish for" sort of story. Except it twisted in the opposite direction from the typical wish tale, which I think makes it kind of charming and fun.

Thresholds of Pain
Writers of speculative fiction tend to love carnivals, sideshows, and other collections of the amazing and the bizarre.

I was thinking about sideshows when it hit me that an alien might fit into one quite nicely. The story gets a bit more graphic than most, and I was a bit worried that I might have gone too far. But I think it's okay. Interestingly enough, right before I did my last revision pass on this book, I saw a sideshow performer drive a nail up his nose.

Smart Food

Since I made fun of vegans in a story a while ago, I figured I should give the vegetables equal time to state their case. After all, everything we eat was once alive. (At least, everything we're supposed to eat. Crayons don't count.) I guess this is as good a time as any to point out that just because I make fun of something doesn't mean I'm against it. I make fun of nerds in lots of my stories, and I'm definitely one myself.

The Art of Alchemy

I came up with the ending first. The hard part was, once I knew what I wanted to have happen, I had to figure out a way to get the characters to a place that had lead, water, and fire. This sort of problem can get tricky. If a writer doesn't do the job well, people will say that the story feels contrived. That's a great word to know, as long as you promise never to use it to describe my stories.

Magnifying the Tragedy

I'm ashamed to admit, given how icky it is, that this is another case where I started with the idea of the ending. Let's leave it at that.

Sweet Dreams

"What if a kid were given some irresistible candy?" That's how it started. Actually, and sadly, there are times when I find all candy to be irresistible. (I try to make sure I'm never left alone with large quantities of peanut butter cups or malted milk balls.) But this was only part of an idea. So what if candy is irresistible? There has to be more at stake. As always, the plot could go in a thousand directions. I'm sure you can think of all sorts of ways, both funny and scary, to write about a character who has a bag of candy she can't keep from eating.

Chipmunks off the Old Block

Chipmunks definitely are goofy. At least, they appear to be goofy. Since I like to turn things around, I figured it would be fun to write a story where the chipmunks turned out to be so brilliant that they appeared to be distracted. I know when I'm deep in thought, I can act goofy or distracted.

Stuck Up

I remember, back when I was in elementary school, kids would talk about what happened if you swallowed your gum. When I was really little, I pictured some sort of gears getting clogged. This story almost ended darkly. When Gilbert was about to cross the street, my first thought was he'd get stuck in traffic. But sometimes, the first thought is a bit too obvious. I like to explore my options—especially when it comes to endings. I'm glad I took the time. Even though it's funny, this ending is also much more horrifying than my first thought. Some of you might wonder whether Gilbert will get rescued by his parents. I guess they'll eventually realize he hasn't come home. But I didn't want to slow down the story by explaining why they weren't around.

The Snow Globe
I came up with the idea of a snow globe that made real snow fall. That, by itself, might not be enough for a story—unless the snow never stopped falling. Happily, a second idea appeared. This happens a lot when I'm thinking about a story and don't feel the idea is strong enough by itself.

The Iron Wizard Goes A-Courtin'
This came straight from the "what-if" file. I pictured a wizard turning to iron so he could walk through fire, and then turning back a bit too soon. As with "The Art of Alchemy," the hard part was setting up the ending. In this case, I had to figure out why he would turn back to flesh so quickly.

Fortunate Accidents
Another serving from the bottomless well of "what if?" The tricky part here was to keep the ending from being obvious. I was pretty sure that some of my readers would expect the rich man to want the kid's heart. I needed to cast doubt in their minds.

Big Bang
I started by wanting to write about someone figuring out the secret of the universe. That, all by itself, doesn't make a very dramatic story. I needed to add another dimension. The universe-ending experiment fit my needs nicely.

Laps

Many years ago, I stayed at the InterContinental Hotel in Chicago for a conference. (My publisher takes me to lots of great places.) The hotel had an old swimming pool. Johnny Weissmuller, who won a bunch of Olympic medals and played Tarzan in the movies, used to train there. Hotel pools always have signs that warn against swimming alone. The memory of the old pool, combined with the signs I've seen so often, gave me the idea for a kid sneaking into a pool. When I started writing, I thought it might become a ghost story. But it went in a different direction.

Bedbugs

Since I speak at schools all over the country, I travel a lot. When the reappearance of bedbugs made the news, it was hard not to think about them. And when I was thinking about bedbugs, I remembered something about another bug. In the summer, my part of Pennsylvania often gets invaded by Japanese beetles. People put out traps that attract the beetles. I realized that if I didn't put any traps out, the beetles would swarm to my neighbors' yards. That thought, turned upside down so the bugs are being repelled rather than attracted, combined nicely with the idea of bedbugs.

The Valley of Lost Treasures

I began with the idea, "What if there's a place where lost toys go?" That changed slightly as I started writing. Instead of toys being lost by all sorts of means, they get lost by going to this place.

Catfishing in America

Several years ago, I was doing an author visit at Schuyler Colfax Middle School in Wayne, New Jersey. During a "what-if" session, one of the students, Bianca Reilly, asked, "What if you had a vampire goldfish?" The instant I heard that, I said, "You'd kill it with a sunfish." That's the nice thing about exciting ideas. They tend to spawn more ideas. I told Bianca that if I ever wrote about sunfish and vampires, I'd give her credit for inspiring me.

Poser

I will sometimes get ideas by coming up with a way of combining different meanings of a word or phrase. It's hard not to notice that a model is both a person who poses and a miniature version of a ship or plane (or anything else). The latter type of model is often made of plastic. In this case, the boy didn't become an actual miniature model. Somehow, I don't think the distinction would make all that much difference to him.

Beware the Ninja Weenies

I'll tell the truth. When I proposed the title, I had no idea what the story would be about, but I knew ninjas would make a great cover. I'm fortunate enough to have met, and even hung out with, several true martial arts masters, so I'm always amused when I see dojos pop up that don't seem to come from an authentic tradition. This was on my mind when I started thinking about the story. Then I did some research, reading about ninjas. I find, if I accumulate enough facts, this will often help me think up a plot. Reading about the things ninjas actually did, such as wearing disguises and creating distractions, definitely guided me toward this story.

Little Bread Riding Hood

This started as a title. Ever since I came up with "The Princess and the Pea Brain," back in the fourth collection (*The Battle of the Red Hot Pepper Weenies*), I've had a fractured fairy tale in each book. It's easy to get ideas by playing with the words in the titles of fairy tales. (I guess I could have written "Little Fred Riding Hood" or "Little Dead Riding Hood." The second one strikes me as an idea that's probably already been used a couple times.) It's also fun and easy to warp a fairy tale, since the story already exists. In this case, I knew she'd be carrying bread (or rolls), and I knew her grandmother would be sick in bed. Beyond that, I just started writing and let things happen.

Gulp

I've toyed with various stories based on the idea of soda (or *pop*, as my friends several states west of here like to say) inside a person who is shaken up. And as faithful Weenies readers know, I'm fond of carnivals as settings for stories. In this case, given that I needed large quantities of soda and some form of violent shaking, a carnival was perfect.

Spring Behind, Fall Ahead

Way back around 1978 (yeah, I'm old), I had an idea for a twist ending for a time-travel story. I wrote the story, but never managed to sell it. (Back then, there were four or five science fiction magazines, and lots of other markets for short stories.) Years later, I took the twist-ending idea, threw out the rest, and wrote a completely different story.

The Garden of Gargoyles

When I was in high school, a friend took me for a ride to this creepy place that had sculptures lining a driveway. It might have been an abandoned monastery. I can't remember the details. But the basic idea of a place lined with statues stayed with me. Eventually, I decided to write about such a place. But gargoyles seemed even better than regular statues.

Alien Biology

As much as I like this story, I had mixed feelings about putting it in the book. After I wrote it, I realized it was similar, in spirit, to one of the most classic and well-known episodes of *The Twilight Zone*. (I won't mention the name of the episode, because that might be enough information to spoil the surprise if you ever see that show.) In the end, I decided it was different enough that I could safely slip it into this collection. As for the inspiration, it came from thinking about the key phrase, *Alien Biology*, and seeing how that could mean different things in different places.

Evil Is in the Eye of the Beholder

My daughter always brings me special presents when she travels. One year, she brought me a teapot shaped like a hand, as a reference to one of my favorite stories of all, "At the Wrist" (from *In the Land of the Lawn Weenies*). She's also given me a gargoyle (which helped inspire another story in this collection), a wonderfully strange mask, and most recently, an evil-eye charm like the one in this story. As I was thinking about how the charm is supposed to work, it hit me that I'd much rather learn to deal with my own envy than protect myself from that of others. And thus was born the idea for the story.

The Dark Side of Brightness

Another from the "what-if" file. I'll admit that I've used whitening strips several times, but I always lose interest before they have any effect. I'd also toyed with dissolved teeth when I was writing the ending of "The Battle of the Red Hot Pepper Weenies," but I decided that was too extreme and permanent a result for the characters in that particular story.

Day Careless

The title popped into my mind. From there, I just started writing. When Jordan reached the basement steps, things turned a bit darker than I'd expected. But then, the plot took another turn. In a typical horror story, Jordan might have come to a bad end in the basement. But the story felt like it needed to go a bit further. I'm glad I took it the extra distance and got the kids out of the basement.

Rat Slayers

I like dungeon-crawling role-playing games. In almost every one of those games with a medieval setting, there's a mission where you have to kill rats in a basement. I liked the idea of writing a story from the viewpoint of an actual game character, without letting the reader know exactly what was going on until the end. In role-playing games, the player has to make lots of decision about which weapons to use, and which skills to develop. For the story, I let the actual player's decision become real experiences for the character.

Frigid Regulations

This was a "what if" for the ending: *What if a girl killed a vampire with a spike of frozen hair?* It wasn't easy figuring out how to set her up with that frozen spike. But it was definitely fun.

Dog Gone

And so we end with another "what-if" question: *What if a vampire used a lost dog to lure victims?* The story "Lost and Found," in an earlier collection, shows the use of a lost object from the viewpoint of the finder. This one gives us the opposite side of the story. I like to end each collection with the scariest story. I'm pretty sure this one does the trick.

Well, I can hardly believe I'm writing the last words for a sixth story collection. Better yet, I'm working on the seventh. I think, by this point, I've pretty much thanked everyone I need to thank, and said, in a half dozen different ways, how fortunate I am to have an audience for my short stories. So let's just leave it with this: I'll see you next time.

READER'S GUIDE

ABOUT THIS GUIDE

The information, activities, and discussion questions that follow are intended to enhance your reading of *Beware the Ninja Weenies*. Please feel free to adapt these materials to suit your needs and interests.

WRITING AND RESEARCH ACTIVITIES

I. Power and Popularity

A. In several stories, characters find themselves in trouble because they follow (for example, "Gorgonzola") or do not follow (for example, "Bed Bugs") a friend's plan. With friends or classmates, discuss a time when you have done something just to follow the crowd. What was the result? What might be some times when it is a good idea to go along with a group? Make a list of stories from *Ninja Weenies*, as well as titles of other books and story collections you have read, that explore the effects of following along with a crowd.

B. In "Catfishing in America" and "Garden of Gargolyes," the main characters force themselves into scary situations by calling another kid's bluff. Create a chart on which to compare and contrast these two stories in terms of the reason the bluff is called, the natural and supernatural elements involved, and the way each plot is resolved.

C. David Lubar concludes "Christmas Carol" with a surprising twist: Carol has not learned any "lesson" from her holiday wish but continues to enjoy endless days of presents. In the character of Carol, write a journal entry describing the day you finally learn a "lesson," what it is, and how (or if) you would wish differently if given the chance.

II. Animals and Aliens

A. From "Flying Solo" to "Alien Biology," many stories feature extraterrestrial beings. Make a chart noting the different extraterrestrials, how they interact with the human characters in the stories, and whether the interaction is helpful, destructive, or has another outcome. Invent an alien to add to the chart, noting how your alien fits into each category.

B. David Lubar comments that he felt "ninja weenies" would look great on a book cover. Review the stories in the collection to find the characters (animal, alien, or otherwise) that paint the most vivid image in your mind's eye. Use colored pencils or paints to create your own, new cover illustration for the book. Write a new title to suit your cover design.

C. Characters in some stories are trying to answer questions, such as where lost objects go, or unlock secrets, such as the mysteries of the universe. Make a list of at least three such stories and then, for each, answer the question, "Does the cliché 'curiosity killed the cat' apply to this story?"

D. From chipmunks to broccoli, some typically voiceless creatures are given their say in this collection. Imagine you have the power to communicate with an animal or object of your choice. Write a one-page, magazine-style interview with this character, including at least five questions to be answered.

III. Story Sources

A. From "Gorgonzola" to "Alchemy," *Ninja Weenies* stories are full of intriguing words that inspired David Lubar's stories. Choose a word with which you are unfamiliar. Go to the library or online to find a definition, information on the word's origin, and more fun facts (e.g., how "gorgonzola" is made or a list of fashion and lifestyle products that use the term "alchemy" in their brand names). On a sheet of 8 ½ x 11" paper, make a miniposter sharing what you have learned. If desired, combine your miniposter with those of friends or classmates to create a display entitled "An Exotic Dictionary Inspired by *Ninja Weenies*."

B. Given David Lubar's penchant for wordplay and twisting clichés, do you think a twisted version of the Golden Rule—*Do a cruel thing unto others and a cruel thing will be done unto you*—could be a theme of this collection? Why or why not? Go to the library or online to find a copy of Benjamin Franklin's *Poor Richard's Almanac* or another book of adages or proverbs. What saying, or twisted version of a saying, would you choose as an organizing idea for this collection? Explain your answer.

C. "What-if's" inspire many of David Lubar's stories. Flip through a newspaper or magazine and write five "what-if questions" about images you see. From your list, select one idea to use as the basis for a short story. First, write a brief outline or concept for your story. Then, take Lubar's advice that "there has to be more at stake" (from his comments on writing "Sweet Dreams") and come up with two ways to raise the stakes for your characters. Finally, write your story and be sure to give it an enticing title.

D. David Lubar credits a middle-school student with inspiring him to write "Catfishing in America." Write a letter to the author, telling him your favorite story from *Ninja Weenies* and suggesting an idea or question that might inspire a new story.

QUESTIONS FOR DISCUSSION

1. *Beware the Ninja Weenies* is David Lubar's sixth Weenie story collection. Have you read other Lubar anthologies, or other story collections? Have you read other scary books? Did you begin reading this book with certain expectations? Explain your answer.
2. We meet the main character of the first story while he is engrossed in playing a video game. Do you think you like video games as much as this kid? Do you ever find yourself getting almost lost in the world of a game? If so, describe this experience.
3. In "Blowout," the main character tells his sister, "There are countless stars. . . . Nobody will miss this one." What characters from other stories do you think have the same sort of philosophy about their actions or powers?

What advice might you give them? Do you think this is a good or bad attitude to have in real life?

4. Compare and contrast the stories in which vampires appear in terms of their relationship to humans, their sense of morality, and their powers. Which story do you feel had the most unique or surprising type of vampire? Explain your answer.

5. "Little Bread Riding Hood" is a fractured—or twisted—version of a classic fairy tale. How does your knowledge of the original "Riding Hood" tale affect your reading of this story? Does it make it funnier or more surprising? What other fairy tale do you think would lend itself well to a "fractured" retelling, and how?

6. Which story or stories in this collection do you think best explore what happens when characters are selfish or lack compassion? Which stories pit the physically or socially weak against the strong or popular? What might you conclude are the best—and safest—qualities and behaviors a kid can have to survive a world of aliens, vampires, and ninja weenies?

7. How are "Evil Is in the Eye of the Beholder," "Thresholds of Pain" and "Day Careless" similar in terms of the main characters' insights into themselves and those they encounter in the story? How might the word "compassion" be used to describe these narrators?

8. Describe the ways video games, television, and other scientific contraptions (such as time machines) are woven into this collection. What conclusions (serious or humorous) might you draw about the care and use of technology after finishing this book?

9. In "The Art of Alchemy," geeky Marvin tells bully Lenny that "anticipation is torture." How does the author use this insight to craft his scary stories? How might you rephrase this observation as a writing tip?

10. In the final line of the final story of the collection, the vampire narrator tells readers, "It's not like I'm some kind of monster." Describe at least two ways this last line could be understood. Who do you think are the worst "monsters" in this story collection? Why do you think David Lubar felt this was the "scariest story" in this anthology?

ABOUT THE AUTHOR

David Lubar grew up in Morristown, New Jersey. His books include *Hidden Talents*, an ALA Best Book for Young Adults; *True Talents*; *Flip*, a VOYA Best Science Fiction, Fantasy, and Horror selection; the Weenies short-story collections *Attack of the Vampire Weenies*, *In the Land of the Lawn Weenies*, *Invasion of the Road Weenies*, *The Curse of the Campfire Weenies*, and *The Battle of the Red Hot Pepper Weenies*; and the Nathan Abercrombie, Accidental Zombie series. He lives in Nazareth, Pennsylvania. You can visit him on the Web at www.davidlubar.com.